Tinker Bell
and
Friends

Book 1

Tink & Lily

First published by Parragon in 2008
Parragon
Queen Street House
4 Queen Street
Bath BA1 1HE, UK

ISBN 978-1-4075-2206-7

Printed in UK

All About Fairies

IF YOU HEAD towards the second star on your right and fly straight on till morning, you'll come to Never Land, a magical island where mermaids play and children never grow up.

When you arrive, you might hear something like the tinkling of little bells. Follow that sound and you'll find Pixie Hollow, the secret heart of Never Land.

A great old maple tree grows in Pixie Hollow and in it live hundreds of fairies and sparrow men. Some of them can do water magic, others can fly like the wind and still others can speak to animals. You see, Pixie Hollow is the Never fairies' kingdom and each fairy who lives there has a special, extraordinary talent.

Not far from the Home Tree, nestled in the branches of a hawthorn, is Mother Dove, the most magical creature of all. She sits on her egg, watching over the fairies, who in turn watch over her. For as long as Mother Dove's egg stays well and whole, no one in Never Land will ever grow old.

Once, Mother Dove's egg *was* broken. But we are not telling the story of the egg here. Now it is time for Tinker Bell's tale. . . .

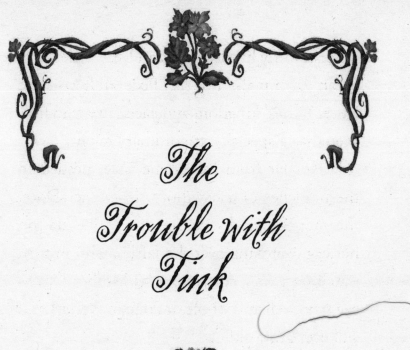

The Trouble with Tink

WRITTEN BY
KIKI THORPE

ILLUSTRATED BY
JUDITH HOLMES CLARKE
& THE DISNEY STORYBOOK ARTISTS

ONE SUNNY, BREEZY afternoon in Pixie
Hollow, Tinker Bell sat in her workshop,
frowning at a copper pot. With one hand she
clutched her tinker's hammer and with the
other she tugged at her blonde fringe, which
was Tink's habit when she was thinking hard
about something. The pot had been squashed
nearly flat on one side. Tink was trying to deter-
mine how to tap it to make it right again.

All around Tink lay her tinkering
tools: baskets full of rivets, scraps of tin,

pliers, iron wire and swatches of steel wool for scouring a pot until it shone. On the walls hung portraits of some of the pans and ladles and washtubs Tink had mended. Tough jobs were always Tink's favourites.

Tink was a pots-and-pans fairy and her greatest joy came from fixing things. She loved anything metal that could be cracked or dented. Even her workshop was made from a tea-kettle that had once belonged to a Clumsy.

Ping! Ping! Ping! Tink began to pound away. Beneath Tink's hammer the copper moved as easily as if she were smoothing the folds in a blanket.

Tink had almost finished when a shadow fell across her work table. She looked up and saw a dark figure silhouetted in the sunny doorway. The edges of the silhouette sparkled.

"Oh, hi, Terence. Come in," said Tink.

Terence moved out of the sunlight and into the room, but he continued to shimmer. Terence was a dust-talent sparrow man. He measured and handed out the fairy dust that allowed Never Land's fairies to fly and do their magic. As a result, he was dustier than most fairies and he sparkled all the time.

"Hi, Tink. Are you working? I mean, I see you're working. Are you almost done? That's a nice pot," Terence said, all in a rush.

"It's Violet's pot. They're dyeing spider silk tomorrow and she needs it for boiling the dye," Tink replied. She looked eagerly at Terence's hands and sighed when she saw that they were empty. Terence stopped by Tink's workshop nearly every day. Often he brought a broken pan or a mangled sieve for her to fix. Other times, like now, he just brought himself.

"That's right, tomorrow is dyeing day,"

said Terence. "I saw the harvest talents bringing in the blueberries for the dye earlier. They've got a good crop this year, they should get a nice deep blue colour . . ."

As Terence rambled on, Tink looked longingly at the copper pot. She picked up her hammer, then reluctantly put it back down. *It would be rude to start tapping right now*, she thought. Tink liked talking to Terence. But she liked tinkering more.

"Anyway, Tink, I just wanted to let you know that they're starting a game of tag in the meadow. I thought maybe you'd like to join in," Terence finished.

Tink's wing tips quivered. It had been ages since there had been a game of fairy tag. Suddenly, she felt herself bursting with the desire to play, the way you fill up with a sneeze just before it explodes.

She glanced down at the pot again. The

dent was nearly smooth. Tink thought she could easily play a game of tag and still have time to finish her work before dinner.

Standing up, she slipped her tinker's hammer into a loop on her belt and smiled at Terence.

"Let's go," she said.

When Tink and Terence got to the meadow, the game of tag was already in full swing. Everywhere spots of bright colour wove in and out of the tall grass as fairies darted after each other.

Fairy tag is different from the sort of tag that humans, or Clumsies, as the fairies call them, play. For one thing, the fairies fly rather than run. For another, the fairies don't just chase each other until one is tagged "it." If that were the case, the fast-flying-talent fairies would win every time.

In fairy tag, the fairies and sparrow men all use their talents to try to win. And when a fairy is tagged, by being tapped on her head and told "Choose you," that fairy's whole talent group – or at least all those who are playing – becomes "chosen." Games of fairy tag are large, complicated and very exciting.

As Tink and Terence joined the game, a huge drop of water came hurtling through the air at them. Terence ducked and the drop splashed against a dandelion behind him. The water-talent fairies were "chosen," Tink realized.

As they sped through the tall grass, the water fairies hurled balls of water at the other fairies. When the balls hit, they burst like water balloons and dampened the fairies' wings. This slowed them down, which helped the water fairies gain on them.

Already the other talents had organized their defence. The animal-talent fairies, led by Beck and Fawn, had rounded up a crew of chipmunks to ride when their wings got too wet to fly. The light-talent fairies bent the sunshine as they flew through it, so rays of light always shone in the eyes of the fairies chasing them. Tink saw that the pots-and-pans fairies had used washtubs to create makeshift catapults. They were trying to catch the balls of water and fling them back at the water fairies.

As Tink zipped down to join them, she heard a voice above her call, "Watch out, Tinker Bell! I'll choose you!" She looked up. Her friend Rani, a water-talent fairy, was circling above her on the back of a dove. Rani was the only fairy in the kingdom who didn't have wings. She'd cut hers off to help save Never Land when Mother Dove's egg had been destroyed. Now Brother Dove did her flying

13

for her.

Rani lifted her arm and hurled a water ball. It wobbled through the air and splashed harmlessly on the ground, inches away from Tink. Tink laughed and so did Rani.

"I'm such a terrible shot!" Rani cried happily.

Just then, the pots-and-pans fairies fired a catapult. The water flew at Rani and drenched her. Rani laughed even harder.

"Choose you!"

The shout rang through the meadow. All the fairies stopped mid-flight and turned. A water-talent fairy named Tally was standing over Jerome, a dust-talent sparrow man. Her hand was on his head.

"Dust talent!" Jerome sang out.

Abruptly, the fairies rearranged themselves. Anyone who happened to be near a dust-talent fairy immediately darted away. The other fairies hovered in the air, waiting to see what the dust talents would do.

Tink caught sight of Terence near a tree stump a few feet away. Terence grinned at her. She coyly smiled back – and then she bolted. In a flash, Terence was after her.

Tink dived into an azalea bush. Terence was right on her heels. Tink's sides ached with laughter, but she kept flying. She wove in and out of the bush's branches. She made a hairpin turn around a thick branch. Then she dashed towards an opening in the leaves and headed back to the open meadow.

But suddenly, the twigs in front of her closed like a gate. Tink skidded to a stop and watched as the twigs wrapped around them-selves. With a flick of fairy dust, Terence had closed the branches of the bush. It was the sim-plest magic. But Tink was trapped.

She turned as Terence flew up to her.

"Choose you," he said, placing his hand on her head. But he said it softly. None of the rest of the fairies could have heard.

Just then, a shout rang out across the meadow: "Hawk!"

At once, Tink and Terence dropped down under the azalea bush's branches. Through the leaves, Tink could see the other fairies ducking for cover. The scout who had spotted the hawk hid in the branches of a nearby elm tree. The entire meadow seemed to hold its breath as the hawk's shadow moved across it.

When it was gone, the fairies waited a few moments, then slowly came out of their hiding places. But the mood had changed. The game of tag was over.

Tink and Terence climbed out of the bush.

"I must finish Violet's pot before dinner," Tink told Terence. "Thank you for telling me about the game."

"I'm really glad you came, Tink," said Terence. He gave her a sparkling smile, but Tink didn't see it. She was already flying away, thinking about the copper pot.

Tink's fingers itched to begin working again. As she neared her workshop, she reached for her tinker's hammer hanging on her belt. Her fingertips touched the leather loop.

Tink stopped flying. Frantically, she ran her fingers over the belt loop again and again. Her hammer was gone.

2

Tink skimmed over the ground, back the way she'd come. Her eyes darted this way and that. She was hoping to catch a glimmer of metal in the tall grass.

"Fool," Tink told herself. "You foolish, foolish fairy."

When she reached the meadow, her heart sank. The trees on the far side of the meadow cast long shadows across the ground. To Tink, the meadow looked huge, like a vast jungle of waving grass and wildflowers. How would she ever find her hammer in there?

Just then, her eyes fell on the azalea bush. *Of course!* Tink thought. *I must have dropped it when I was dodging Terence.*

Tink flew to the bush. She checked the ground beneath it and checked each branch. She paid particular attention to the places where a pots-and-pans fairy's hammer might get caught. Then she checked them again. And again. But the hammer was nowhere in sight.

Fighting back tears, Tink flew across the open meadow. She tried to recall her zigzagging path in the tag game. Eventually she gave that up and began to search the meadow inch by inch, flying close to the ground. She parted the petals of wildflowers. She peered into rabbit burrows. She looked everywhere she could think of, even places she knew the hammer couldn't possibly be.

As Tink searched, the sun sank into a red

pool on the horizon, then disappeared. A thin sliver of moon rose in the sky. The night was so dark that even if Tink had flown over the hammer, she wouldn't have been able to see it. But the hammer was already long gone. A Never crow had spotted it hours before and, attracted by its shine, had carried it off to its nest.

The grass was heavy with dew by the time Tink slowly started back to the Home Tree. As she flew, tears of frustration rolled down her cheeks. She swiped them away. *What will I do without my hammer?* Tink wondered. It was her most important tool. She thought of the copper pot waiting patiently for her in her workshop and more tears sprang to her eyes.

It might seem that it should have been easy for Tink to get another tinker's hammer, but in fact, it was not. In the fairy kingdom, there is just the right amount of everything;

no more, no less. A tool-making fairy would need Never iron to make a new hammer. And a mining-talent fairy would have to collect the iron. Because their work was difficult, the mining-talent fairies only mined once in a moon cycle, when the moon was full. Tink eyed the thin silver slice in the sky. Judging from the moon, that wouldn't be for many days.

For a pots-and-pans fairy, going many days without fixing pots or pans would be like not eating or sleeping. To Tink, the idea was horrible.

But that wasn't the only reason she was crying. Tink had a secret. She *did* have a spare hammer. But it was at Peter Pan's hideout – she had accidentally left it there quite a while before. And she was terribly scared about going back to get it.

Tink got back to the Home Tree, but she was too upset to go inside and sleep. Instead, she flew up to the highest branch and perched there. She looked up at the stars and tried to figure out what to do.

Tink thought about Peter Pan: his wild red hair, his freckled nose turned up just so, his eyes that looked so happy when he laughed. She remembered the time that she and Peter had gone to the beach to skim rocks on the lagoon. One of the rocks had accidentally nicked a mermaid's tail as she dived beneath the water. The mermaid had scolded them so ferociously that Peter and Tink had fled laughing all the way to the other side of the island.

Tink's heart ached. Remembering Peter Pan was something she almost never let herself do. Since he had brought the Wendy to Never Land, Tink and Peter had hardly spoken.

No, Tink decided. She couldn't go to Peter's for the spare hammer. It would make her too sad.

"I'll make do without it," she told herself. What was a hammer, after all, but just another tool?

3

Tink slept fitfully that night and woke before the other fairies. As the sky began to get lighter, she crept out of the Home Tree and flew down to the beach.

In one corner of the lagoon, there was a small cave that could only be entered at low tide. Tink flew in and landed on the damp ground. The floor of the cave was covered with sea-polished pebbles. This was where Peter had come to get stones for skimming on the water, Tink remembered.

Tink carefully picked her way through the rocks. Many of them were as big as her head. They were all smooth and shiny with seawater.

At last, Tink picked up a reddish pebble the size and shape of a sunflower seed. She threw it once into the air and caught it again.

"This might work," Tink said aloud into the empty cave.

Might work, her voice echoed back to her.

As the tide rose and the waves began to roll in, Tink flew out of the cave, gripping the pebble in her fist.

Back in her workshop, Tink used iron wire to bind the flat side of the rock to a twig. With a pinch of fairy dust, she tightened the wires so the rock was snug against the wood. She held up her makeshift hammer and looked at it.

"It's not so bad," she said. She tried to sound positive.

Taking a deep breath, Tink began to tap the copper pot.

Clank! Clank! Clank! Tink winced as the horrible sound echoed through her workshop. With each blow, the copper pot seemed to shudder.

"I'm sorry, I'm sorry!" Tink whispered to the pot. She tried to tap more gently.

The work took forever. Each strike with the pebble hammer left a tiny dent. Slowly, the bent copper straightened out. But the pot's smooth, shiny surface was now as pitted and pockmarked as the skin of a grapefruit.

Tink fought back tears. *It's no good*, she thought. *This pebble doesn't work at all!*

Tink raised her arm to give the pot one last tap. Just then, the pebble flew off the stick and landed with a clatter in a pile of tin scrap, as if to say it agreed.

Suddenly, the door of Tink's workshop burst open and a fairy flew in. She wore a gauzy dress tie-dyed in a fancy pattern of blues and greens. Her cheeks were bright splotches of pink. Corkscrews of curly red hair stood out in all directions from her head and her hands were stained purple with berry juice. She looked as if she had been painted using all the colours in a watercolour box. It was Violet, the pot's owner, a dyeing-talent fairy.

"Tink! Thank goodness you're almost done with the . . . Oh!" Violet exclaimed. She stopped and stared. Tink was standing over the copper pot, gripping a twig as if she planned to beat it like a drum.

"Oh, Violet, hi. Yes, I'm, er . . . I'm done with the pot. That is, mostly," Tink said. She put down the twig. With the other hand, she tugged nervously at her fringe.

"It looks . . . uh . . ." Violet's voice trailed off as she eyed the battered pot. Tink was the best pots-and-pans fairy in the kingdom. Violet didn't want to sound as if she was criticizing her work.

"It needs a couple of touch-ups, but I fixed the squashed part," Tink reassured her. "It's perfectly good for boiling dye in. We can try it now if you like."

The door of Tink's workshop opened again. Terence came in, carrying a ladle that was so twisted it looked as if it had been tied in a knot.

"Hi, Tink! I brought you a ladle to fix!" he called out. "Oh, hello, Violet! Dropping off?" he asked as he spied the copper pot.

"No . . . er, picking up," Violet said worriedly.

"Oh," said Terence. He looked back at the pot in surprise.

Tink filled a bucket with water from a rain barrel outside her workshop and brought it over to her work table. As Violet and Terence watched, she poured the water into the copper pot.

"See?" Tink said to Violet. "It's good as –"

Just then, they heard a metallic creaking sound. Suddenly – *plink, plink, plink, plink!* One by one, tiny streams of water burst through the damaged copper. The pot looked more like a watering can than something to boil dye in.

"Oh!" Violet and Terence gasped. They turned to Tink, their eyes wide.

Tink felt herself blush, but she couldn't tear her eyes away from the leaking pot. She had never failed to fix a pot before, much less made it worse than it was when she got it.

The thing was, no fairy ever failed at her talent. To do so would mean you weren't really talented at all.

AFTER A LONG, awkward silence, Violet closed her mouth, cleared her throat and said, "I can probably share a dye pot with someone else. I'll come back and get this later." With a last confused glance at Tink, she hurried out of the door.

Terence was also confused, but he was in no hurry to leave. He set the twisted ladle down on Tink's workbench.

"Tink, you look tired," he said gently.

"I'm not tired," said Tink.

"Maybe you need to take a break," Terence suggested. But he wasn't at all sure what Tink needed. "Why don't we fly to the tearoom? On my way here, I smelled pumpkin muffins baking in the kitchen. They smelled deli –"

"I'm not hungry," Tink interrupted, although she was starving. She hadn't had breakfast, or dinner the night before. But the talents always sat together in the tearoom. Tink didn't feel like sitting at a table with the other pots-and-pans fairies right now.

Suddenly, Tink was irritated with Terence. If he hadn't told her about the tag game, she never would have lost her hammer. Tink knew she wasn't being fair. But she was upset and embarrassed, and she wanted someone to blame.

"I can't talk today, Terence," she snapped. She turned towards a pile of baking tins that needed repair and tugged at her fringe. "I have a lot of work and I'm already behind."

"Oh." Terence's shoulders sagged. "Just let me know if you need anything," he said, and headed for the door. "Bye, Tink."

As soon as Terence was gone, Tink flew to a nearby birch tree where a carpenter-talent sparrow man worked and asked if she could borrow his hammer. The sparrow man agreed, provided that she brought it back in two days' time. He was in the middle of cutting oak slats for some repairs in the Home Tree, he said, and wouldn't need the hammer until he was through. Tink promised she would.

Two days. Tink didn't know what she'd do after that. But she wasn't going to think about it, she decided. Not just yet.

When Tink entered her empty workshop, something seemed different. There was a sweet smell in the air. Then she spied a plate with a pumpkin muffin on it and a cup of buttermilk on her workbench.

Terence, Tink thought. She was sorry that she'd snapped at him earlier.

The muffin was moist, sweet and still warm from the oven, and it melted on her tongue. The buttermilk was cool and tart. As soon as she'd eaten, Tink felt better.

She picked up the carpenter's hammer and began work on a stack of pie pans. The pans weren't cracked or dented, but Dulcie, the baking-talent fairy who'd brought them to her, complained that the pies she baked in them kept burning. Tink thought it had something to do with the pans' shape, or maybe the tin on the bottom of the pans was too thin.

The carpenter's hammer was almost twice as big as her tinker's hammer. Holding it in her hand, Tink felt as clumsy as a Clumsy.

Still, she had to admit that it was much better than the pebble.

Tink worked slowly with the awkward hammer. She reshaped the pie pans, then added an extra layer of tin to the bottom of each one. When she was done, she looked over her work.

It's not the best job I've ever done, she thought. *But it's not so bad, either.*

Tink gathered the pie pans into a stack and carried them to Dulcie. Dulcie was delighted to have them back.

"Don't miss tea this afternoon, Tink," she said with a wink as she brushed flour from her hands. "We're making strawberry pie. I'll save you an extra-big slice!"

On the way back to her workshop, Tink ran into Prilla, a young fairy with a freckled nose and a bouncy nature. Prilla always did cartwheels and handsprings when she was excited about something.

"Tink!" Prilla cried, bounding over to her.

"Did you hear?"

"Hear what?" asked Tink.

"About Queen Ree's tub," Prilla told her. Ree was the fairies' nickname for their queen, Clarion. "It's sprung a leak. The queen's whole bath trickled out while she was washing this morning."

Tink's eyes widened. The bathtub was one of Queen Ree's most prized possessions. It was the size of a coconut shell and made of Never pewter, with morning glory leaves sculpted into its sides. The tub rested on four feet shaped like lions' paws and there were two notches at the back where the queen could rest her wings to keep them dry while she took her bath.

Tink's fingers twitched. She would love to work on the bathtub.

"The queen's attendants looked all over, but they couldn't spot the leak. I thought of you when I heard, Tink," Prilla said. "Of course,

Queen Ree will want you to fix it. You're the best." Prilla grinned at Tink and did a hand-spring.

Tink grinned back, showing her deep dimples. It was the first time she'd smiled since she lost her hammer. "I hope so, Prilla. It would be quite an honour to work on the queen's tub," she replied.

Prilla turned a one-handed cartwheel and flew on. "See you later, Tink!" she called.

Tink thought about the queen's tub all afternoon as she fixed the spout on a tea-kettle that wouldn't whistle. What kind of leak could it be? A hairline crack? Or a pinprick hole? Tink smiled, imagining the possibilities.

By the time Tink had finished fixing the kettle, it was nearly teatime.

"They'll need this in the kitchen," Tink said to herself as she buffed the tea-kettle with a piece of suede. She would take it to the kitchen, then go to the tearoom for strawberry pie. Tink's stomach rumbled hungrily at the thought. Strawberry was one of her favourite kinds of pie.

But when she got to the kitchen, a horrible smell greeted her. Tink quickly handed the tea-kettle to one of the cooking-talent fairies and held both hands to her nose. "What is that smell?" she asked the fairy. "It's not strawberry pie."

But the fairy just gave her a strange look and hurried off to fill the tea-kettle with water.

Tink made her way through the kitchen until she found Dulcie. She was standing over several steaming pies that had just been pulled from the oven. She looked as if she might cry.

"Dulcie, what's going on?" Tink asked.

As soon as Dulcie saw Tink, her forehead wrinkled. The wrinkles made little creases in the flour on her skin, which made the lines seem even deeper.

"Oh, Tink. I don't know how to tell you this," Dulcie said. "It's the pies. They're all coming out mincemeat."

Tink turned and looked at the steaming pies. That was where the horrible smell was coming from.

"We tried everything," Dulcie went on. "When the strawberry came out all wrong, we tried plum. When that didn't work, we tried cherry. We even tried pumpkin. But every time we pulled the pies out of the oven, they'd turned into mincemeat." Now Dulcie's chin wrinkled like a walnut as she struggled to hold back tears. Her whole face was puckered with worry.

This was indeed a kitchen disaster. Fairies hate mincemeat. To them it tastes like burned broccoli and old socks.

"Is there something wrong with the oven?"

Tink asked Dulcie. She didn't know much about ovens. But if there was something metal in it, she could probably fix it.

Dulcie swallowed hard.

"No, Tink," she said. "It's the pans you fixed. Only the pies baked in those pans are the ones that get spoiled."

5

Tɪɴᴋ'ꜱ ᴍɪɴᴅ ʀᴇᴇʟᴇᴅ. She took a step back from Dulcie. But before she could say anything, a shrill whistle split the air.

The tea water had boiled. A cooking-talent sparrow man hurried over to lift the kettle off the fire. Expertly, the sparrow man poured the water into the teacups until there wasn't a drop left.

But the tea-kettle continued to shriek. The sparrow man lifted the kettle's lid to let out any steam that might have been caught inside. A puff of steam escaped, but the kettle still whistled on. Without pausing, it changed pitch and began to whistle a lively, ear-splitting melody.

All the fairies in the kitchen, including Tink, covered their ears. Several fairies from other talents who were in the tearoom poked their heads in the door of the kitchen.

"What's all that noise?" a garden-talent fairy asked one of the baking-talent fairies.

"It's the tea-kettle, the one that just wouldn't whistle," the baking-talent fairy replied. She winced as the kettle hit a particularly high note. "Tink fixed it and now it won't shut up!"

Twee-twee-tweeeeeeeeee! the tea-kettle shrieked cheerfully, as if confirming that what she'd said was true. The fairies cringed and clamped their hands more tightly against their ears.

"And the pie pans Tink fixed aren't any good, either," another baking-talent fairy noted over the noise. "Every pie baked in them turns into mincemeat!"

A murmur went around the room. *What could this mean?* the other fairies wondered. *Was it some kind of bad joke?* Everyone turned and looked at Tink.

Tink stared back at them, blushing so deeply her glow turned orange. Then, without thinking, she turned and fled.

Tink was sitting in the shade of a wild rosebush, deep in thought. She didn't notice Vidia, a fast-flying-talent fairy, flying overhead. Suddenly, Vidia landed right in front of Tink.

"Tinker Bell, darling," Vidia greeted her.

"Hello, Vidia," Tink replied. Of all the fairies in the kingdom, Vidia was the one Tink liked the least. Vidia was pretty, with her long dark hair, arched eyebrows and pouting lips. But she was selfish and mean-spirited, and at the moment she was smiling in a way Tink didn't like at all.

"I'm so *sorry* to hear about your trouble, Tink darling," Vidia said.

"It's nothing," Tink said. "I was just flustered. I'll go back to the kitchen and fix the tea-kettle now."

"Oh, don't worry about that. Angus was in the tearoom," Vidia said. Angus was a pots-and-pans sparrow man. "He got the tea-kettle to shut up. No, Tink, what I meant was, I'm sorry to hear about your *talent*."

Tink blinked. "What do you mean?"

"Oh, don't you know?" Vidia asked. "Everyone's talking about it. The rumour flying around the kingdom, Tink dear, is that you've lost your talent."

"What?" Tink leaped to her feet.

"Oh, it's such a *shame*, dearest," Vidia went on, shaking her head. "You were always such a good little tinker."

"I haven't lost my talent," Tink growled. Her cheeks were burning. Her hands were balled into fists.

"If you say so. But, sweetheart, you have to admit, your work hasn't exactly been . . . *inspired* lately. Why, even I could fix pots and pans better than that," Vidia said with a little laugh. "But I wouldn't worry too much. I'm sure they won't make you leave the fairy kingdom *forever*, even if your talent has dried up for good."

Tink looked at her coldly. *I wish* you *would leave forever*, she thought. But she wasn't going to give Vidia the satisfaction of seeing that she was mad. Instead, she said, "I'm sure that would never happen, Vidia."

"Yes." Vidia gave Tink a pitying smile. "But no one really knows, do they? After all, no fairy has ever lost her talent before. But I guess we'll soon find out. You see, dear heart, I've come with a message. The queen would like to see you."

Tink's stomach did a little flip. The queen?

"She's in the gazebo," Vidia told her. "I'll let you fly there on your own. I expect you'll want to collect your thoughts. Goodbye, Tink." With a last sugary smile, Vidia flew away.

Tink's heart raced. What could this mean? Was it really possible that she could be banished from the kingdom for losing her talent?

But I haven't lost my talent! Tink thought indignantly. *I've just lost my hammer.*

With that thought in mind, Tink took a deep breath, lifted her chin and flew off to meet the queen.

As she made her way to the gazebo, Tink passed a group of harvest-talent fairies filling wheelbarrows with sunflower seeds to take to the kitchen. They laughed and chatted as they worked, but as soon as they saw Tink, they all stopped talking. Silently, they watched her go by. Tink could have sworn she heard one of them whisper the word "talent."

So it's true, Tink thought. *Everyone is saying I've lost my talent.*

Tink scowled as she flew past another

group of fairies who silently gawped at her. She had always hated gossip and now she hated it even more.

The queen's gazebo sat high on a rock overlooking the fairy kingdom. Tink landed lightly on a bed of soft moss outside the entrance. All around her she heard the jingle of seashell wind chimes, which hung around the gazebo.

Inside, the gazebo was drenched in purple from the sunlight filtering through the violet petals that made up the roof. Soft, fresh fir needles carpeted the floor and gave off a piney scent.

Queen Ree stood at one of the open windows. She was looking out at the glittering blue water of the Mermaid Lagoon, which lay in the distance beyond the fairy kingdom. When she heard Tink, she turned.

"Tinker Bell, come in," said the queen.

Tink stepped inside. She waited.

"Tink, how are you feeling?" Queen Ree asked.

"I'm fine," Tink replied.

"Are you sleeping well?" asked the queen.

"Well enough," Tink told her. *Except for last night*, she added to herself. But she didn't feel the need to tell this to the queen.

"No cough? Your glow hasn't changed colour?" asked the queen.

"No," Tink replied. Suddenly, she realized that the queen was checking her for signs of fairy distemper. It was a rare illness, but very contagious. If Tink had it, she would have to be separated from the group to keep from making the whole fairy kingdom sick. "No, I'm fine," Tink repeated to reassure her. "I feel very well. Really."

When the queen heard this, she seemed to relax. It was just the slightest change in her posture, but Tink noticed and she, too, breathed a sigh of relief. Queen Ree would not banish her, Tink realized. The queen would never make such a hasty or unfair decision. It had been mean and spiteful of Vidia to say such a thing.

"Tink, you know there are rumours...." Queen Ree hesitated. She was reluctant to repeat them.

"They say I've lost my talent," Tink said quickly so that the queen wouldn't have to. "It's nasty gossip – and untrue. It's just that –" Tink stopped. She tugged at her fringe.

She was afraid that if she told Queen Ree about her missing hammer, the queen would think she was irresponsible.

Queen Ree waited for Tink to go on. When she didn't, the queen walked closer to her and looked into her blue eyes. "Tink," she said, "is there anything you want to tell me?"

She asked so gently that Tink felt the urge

to plop down on the soft fir needles and tell her everything – about the pebble hammer and the carpenter's hammer and even about Peter Pan. But Tink had never told another fairy about Peter and she was afraid to now.

Besides, Tink told herself, *the queen has more important things to worry about than a missing hammer.*

Tink shook her head. "No," she said. "I'm sorry my pots and pans haven't been very good lately. I'll try to do better."

Queen Ree looked carefully at her. She knew something was wrong, but she didn't know what. She only knew that Tink didn't want to tell her. "Very well," she said. As Tink turned to leave, she added, "Be good to yourself, Tink."

Outside, Tink felt better. The meeting with the queen had been nothing to worry about at all. Maybe things weren't as bad as they seemed.

All I have to do now is find a new hammer and everything will be back to normal, Tink thought with a burst of confidence.

"Tink!" someone called.

She looked down and saw Rani and Prilla standing knee-deep in a puddle. Tink flew down and landed at the edge.

"What are you doing?" she asked, eyeing the fairies' wet clothes and hair. She was used to seeing Rani in the water. But Prilla wasn't a water fairy.

"Rani's showing me how she makes fountains in the water," Prilla explained. "I want to learn. I thought it might be fun to try in Clumsy children's lemonade." Prilla's talent was travelling over to the mainland in the blink of an eye and visiting the children there. She was the only fairy in all of Never Land who had this talent and it was an important one. She helped keep up children's belief in fairies, which in turn saved the fairies' lives.

Tink looked at the drenched hem of Prilla's long dress and shivered. She didn't like to get wet – it always made her feel cold. She was surprised that Prilla could stand to be in the water for so long.

"I've been trying all afternoon, but this is all I can do," Prilla told her. She took a pinch of fairy dust and sprinkled it onto the water. Then she stared hard at the spot where the dust had landed and concentrated with all her might. After a moment, a few small bubbles rose to the surface and popped.

"Like a tadpole burping," Prilla said with a sigh. "Now watch Rani."

Rani sprinkled a pinch of fairy dust on the water, then stared at the spot where it had landed. Instantly, a twelve-inch fountain of water shot up from the puddle.

Tink and Prilla clapped their hands and

cheered. "If I could make just a teeny little fountain, I'd be happy," Prilla confessed to Tink. Tink nodded, though she didn't really understand. She'd never wanted to make a water fountain.

Just then, Tink heard a snuffling sound. She turned and saw that Rani was crying.

"I'm so sorry, Tink," Rani said. She pulled a damp leaf kerchief from one of her many pockets and blew her nose into it. As a water fairy, Rani cried a lot and was always prepared. "About your talent, I mean."

Tink's smile faded. She tugged at her fringe. "There's nothing to be sorry about. There's nothing wrong with my talent," she said irritably.

"Don't worry, Tink," Prilla said. "I know how you feel. When I thought I didn't have a talent, it was awful." Prilla hadn't known what her talent was when she first arrived in Never Land. She'd had to figure it out on her own. "Maybe you just need to try lots of things," she advised Tink, "and then it will come to you."

"I already have a talent, Prilla," Tink said carefully.

"But maybe you need another talent, like a backup when the one you have isn't working," Prilla went on. "You could learn to make fountains with me. Rani will teach you, too, won't you, Rani?"

Rani sniffled helplessly. Tink tugged her fringe so hard that a few blond hairs came out in her fingers. What Prilla was suggesting sounded crazy to Tink. She had never wanted to do anything but fix pots and pans.

"Anyway, Tink," said Prilla, "I wouldn't worry too much about what everyone is saying about –"

"Dinner?" Rani cut Prilla off.

Prilla looked at her. "No, I meant –"

"Yes, about dinner," Rani interrupted again, more firmly. She had dried her eyes and now she was looking hard at Prilla. Rani could see that the topic of talents was upsetting Tink and she wanted Prilla to be quiet. "It's time, isn't it?"

"Yes," said Tink. But she wasn't looking at Rani and Prilla. Her mind seemed to be somewhere else altogether.

Rani put her fingers to her mouth and whistled. They heard the sound of wings beating overhead. A moment later, Brother Dove landed on the ground next to Rani. He would take her to the tearoom.

But before Rani had even climbed onto his back, Tink took off in the direction of the Home Tree without another word. Rani and Prilla had no choice but to follow.

7

WHEN THEY REACHED the tearoom, Tink said goodbye to Rani and Prilla. Rani was going to sit with the other water-talent fairies and Prilla was joining her. Since Prilla didn't have her own talent group, she was an honorary member of many different talents and she sat at a different table every night. Tonight she would sit with the water-talent fairies and practise making fountains in her soup.

Tink made her way over to a table under a large chandelier where the pots-and-pans fairies sat together for their meals. As she took her seat, the other fairies at the table barely looked up.

"It's a crack in the bottom, I'll bet," a fairy named Zuzu was saying. "I mended a pewter bowl once that had boiling water poured in it when it was cold. A crack had formed right down the centre." Her eyes glazed over happily as she recalled fixing the bowl.

"But don't you think it could be something around the drain, since the water leaked out so quickly?" asked Angus, the sparrow man who had fixed the whistling tea-kettle in the kitchen earlier that day.

A serving-talent fairy with a large soup tureen walked over to the table and began to ladle chestnut dumpling soup into the fairies' bowls. Tink noticed with pride that the ladle was one she had once repaired.

She leaned forwards. "What's everyone talking about?" she asked the rest of the table.

The other fairies turned, as if noticing for the first time that Tink was sitting there.

"About Queen Ree's bathtub," Zuzu explained. "She's asked us to come fix it tomorrow. We're trying to guess what's wrong with it."

"Oh, yes!" said Tink. "I've been thinking about that, too. It might be a pinprick hole. Those are the sneakiest sorts of leaks – the water just sort of drizzles out one drop at a time." Tink laughed.

But no one joined her. She looked around the table. The other fairies were staring at her, or looking awkwardly down at their soup bowls. Suddenly, Tink realized that the queen had said nothing to her about the bathtub that afternoon in the gazebo.

"Tink," another fairy named Copper said gently, "we've all agreed that Angus and Zuzu should be the ones to repair the tub, since they are the most talented pots-and-pans fairies . . . lately, that is."

"Oh!" said Tink. "Of course." She swallowed hard. She felt as if a whole chestnut dumpling were stuck in her throat.

Now all the pots-and-pans fairies were looking at Tink with a mixture of love and concern. And, Tink was sad to see, pity.

I could just tell everyone that I lost my hammer, Tink thought. *But if they asked about the spare* . . .

Tink couldn't finish the thought. For a long, long time, Tink had neglected her pots and pans to spend all her time with Peter Pan. It was something she thought the other pots-and-pans fairies would never understand.

At last the fairies changed the topic and began to talk about the leaky pots and broken tea kettles they'd fixed that day. As they chattered and laughed, Tink silently ate her soup.

Nearby, a cheer went up from the water fairies' table. Tink looked over and saw that Prilla had succeeded in making a tiny fountain in her soup.

Prilla has two talents now, Tink thought glumly. *And I haven't even got one.*

As soon as she was done with her soup, Tink put down her spoon and slipped away from the table. The other pots-and-pans fairies were so busy talking, they didn't notice her leaving.

Outside, Tink returned to the topmost branches of the Home Tree, where she'd sat the night before. She didn't want to go back to her workshop – there were pots and pans still waiting to be fixed. She didn't want to go to her room, either. It seemed too lonely there. At least here she had the stars to keep her company.

"Maybe it's true that I've lost my talent," Tink said to the stars. "If I don't have a hammer, then I can't fix things. And if I can't fix things, it's just like having no talent at all."

The stars only twinkled in reply.

From where she was sitting, Tink could see the hawthorn tree where Mother Dove lived. Between its branches, she could make out the faint shape of Mother Dove's nest. Mother Dove was the only creature in the fairy kingdom who knew all about Tink and Peter Pan. Once, after the hurricane that broke Mother Dove's wings and nearly destroyed Never Land, Tink had sat on the beach with Mother Dove and told her tales of her adventures with Peter. She had also told Mother Dove about the Wendy and how when she came to Never Land, Peter forgot all about Tink.

What a comfort it would be to go to Mother Dove. She would know what to do.

But something held Tink back. She remembered Mother Dove's words to her on her very first day in Never Land: *You're Tinker Bell, sound and fine as a bell. Shiny and jaunty as a new pot. Brave enough for anything, the most courageous fairy to come in a long year.* Tink had felt so proud that day.

But Tink didn't feel very brave right now, certainly not brave enough to go to Peter's and get her spare hammer. He was only a boy, but still she couldn't find the courage.

Tink couldn't bear the idea that Mother Dove would think she wasn't brave or sound or fine. It would be worse than losing her talent.

"Tink," said a voice.

Tink turned. Terence was standing behind her on the branch. She'd been so wrapped up in her thoughts, she hadn't even heard him fly up.

"I haven't fixed the ladle yet," Tink told him miserably.

"I didn't come because of the ladle," Terence replied. "I saw you leave the tearoom."

When Tink didn't explain, Terence sat down next to her on the branch. "Tink, are you all right? Everyone is saying that . . ." He paused. Like Queen Ree, Terence couldn't bring himself to repeat the gossip. It seemed too unkind.

"That I've lost my talent," Tink finished for him. She sighed. "Maybe they're right, Terence. I can't seem to fix anything. Everything I touch comes out worse than when I started."

Terence was startled. One thing he had always admired about Tink was her fierceness: her fierce dark eyebrows, her fierce determination, even the fierce happiness of her dimpled smile. He had never seen her look as defeated as she did now.

"I don't believe that," he told her. "You're the best pots-and-pans fairy in the kingdom. Talent doesn't just go away like that."

Tink said nothing. But she felt grateful to him for not believing the rumours. For still believing in her.

"Tink," Terence asked gently, "what's really going on?"

Tink hesitated. "I lost my hammer," she blurted at last.

As soon as the words left her lips, Tink felt relieved. It was as if she'd let out a huge breath that she'd been holding in.

"Is that all it is?" Terence said. He almost laughed. It seemed like such a small thing. "But you could borrow a hammer," he suggested.

Tink told Terence about the hammer

she'd made from a pebble and the one she'd borrowed from the carpenter fairy. "Neither of them works," she explained. "I need a tinker's hammer."

"Maybe there's a spare –" Terence began.

"I *have* a spare," Tink wailed. She'd already been over this so many times in her own mind. "But it's . . . I . . . I left it at Peter Pan's hide-out."

"He won't give it back?" asked Terence.

Tink shook her head. "I haven't asked." She looked away.

Terence didn't know much about Peter Pan, only that Tink had been friends with him and then – suddenly – she wasn't. But he saw that Tink was upset and ashamed so he didn't ask her anything more. Again, Tink felt a surge of gratitude towards him.

They sat silently for a moment, looking up at the stars.

"I could go with you," Terence said at last. "To Peter Pan's, I mean."

Tink's mind raced. Perhaps if someone else came along, it wouldn't be so hard to see Peter. . . .

"You would do that?" she asked.

"Tink," said Terence, "I'm your friend. You don't even need to ask."

He gave Tink a sparkling smile. This time, Tink saw it and she smiled back.

8

EARLY THE NEXT morning, before most of
the fairy kingdom was awake, Tink rapped at
the door of Terence's room. She wanted to
leave for Peter's hideout before she lost her
nerve altogether.

Terence threw open the door after the
first knock. He grinned at Tink. "Ready to go
get your talent back, Tinker Bell?"

Tink smiled. She was glad Terence was
going with her, and not just because it would
be easier with someone else along.

They left Pixie Hollow just as the sun's rays shone over Torth Mountain. They flew over the banana farms, where the Tiffens were already out working in the fields. In the distance, they could hear the laughter of the mermaids in the lagoon.

"See that peak?" Tink told Terence. She pointed out a chair-shaped spot at the top of a hill. "That's called the Throne. When the Lost Boys have their skirmishes, the winner is named king of the hill. Of course, if Peter is there, he always wins. The Lost Boys wouldn't dare to beat him, even if they could," Tink explained.

"And that stream," she went on, pointing to a silver ribbon of water winding through the forest below, "leads to an underground cavern that's filled with gold and silver. Captain Hook and his men have hidden away a whole pirate ship's worth of treasure there."

Tink remembered how she had found the cavern. She had been racing along the stream in a little birch-bark canoe Peter had made for her. Peter had been running along the bank. When the stream suddenly dived underground, Tink had plunged right along with it. Peter had been so thrilled with her discovery that Tink hadn't even minded the soaking she got when the canoe splashed down in the cavern.

"You must know Never Land better than any fairy in the kingdom," Terence said admiringly.

Tink looked at the island below her and felt a little twinge of pride. What Terence said was true. With Peter, Tink had explored nearly every inch of Never Land. Every rock, meadow and hill reminded her of some adventure.

Of course, they also reminded her of Peter.

Tink felt a flutter of nervousness. How

would it be to see him? What if the Wendy was there, or Peter had found someone else to play with? What if he ignored her again?

Tink fell silent. Terence, sensing that something bothered her, said nothing more for the rest of their trip.

When Tink reached the densest, darkest part of the forest, she began to glide down in a spiral. Terence followed her.

They plunged through a canopy of fig trees and landed on a white-speckled mushroom. The mushroom was nearly as wide as a Clumsy's dinner plate. Terence was surprised to feel that it was quite warm.

"It's Peter's hideout," Tink explained. "They use a mushroom cap to disguise the chimney to fool Captain Hook."

After they'd rested for a moment, Tink sprang from the mushroom and flew up to a hollow in the trunk of a nearby jackfruit tree.

She was about to dive inside when Terence grabbed her wrist.

"What about owls?" he said worriedly. If there was an owl living in the hollow, it might eat them.

Tink laughed. "Anything that lived here would be terrorized by the Lost Boys. This is the entrance to the hideout!"

Peeking inside, Terence saw the entire tree was hollow, right to its roots. He followed Tink as she flew down the trunk. They came out in an underground room.

Terence looked around. The floor and walls were made of packed earth. Tree roots hung down from the ceiling and, from these, string hammocks dangled limply. Here and there on the ground lay slingshots, socks and dirty coconut-shell bowls. The remains of a fire smouldered in a corner. The whole place had the dry, puppyish smell of little boys.

But there were no little boys in sight. The hideout was empty.

He's not home, Tink thought. She felt both disappointed and relieved.

Just then, they heard whistling coming from somewhere near the back of the den.

Tink and Terence flew towards the sound. Their glows made two bright spots of light in the dim room.

At the back of the hideout, they spied a nook that was tucked out of sight from the rest of the room. The whistling was coming from there.

When they rounded the corner, Terence saw a freckled boy with a mop of red hair sitting on a stool formed by a thick, twisted root. In one hand he held a jackknife and he whistled as he worked it over a piece of wood. A fishing rod leaned against the wall behind him. Looking more closely, Terence saw that the boy was carving a fishing hook big enough to catch a whale.

Tink saw her old friend, Peter Pan.

Taking a deep breath, Tink said, "Hello, Peter."

But Peter didn't seem to hear her. He continued to whistle and chip at the wood.

Tink flew a little bit closer. "Peter!" she exclaimed.

Peter kept on whistling and whittling.

Was he deaf? Or could he be angry with her? Tink wondered with a sudden shock. The thought had never occurred to her. She hovered, unsure what to do.

Then Terence took her hand. They flew up to Peter until they were just a few inches from his face. "Peter!" they both cried.

Peter lifted his head. When he saw them, a bright smile lit his face.

Tink smiled, too.

"Hello! What's this?" Peter said. He looked back and forth between the fairies. "Two butterflies have come to visit me! Are you lost, butterflies?"

Tink's smile faded. She and Terence stared at Peter. *Butterflies?*

Tink thought, *Has he forgotten me already?*

Peter squinted at them and whistled low. "You're awful pretty. I just love butterflies," he said. "You'd make a fine addition to my collection. Let's see now, where are my pins?"

He began to search his pockets. As he did, small items fell onto the ground beneath his seat: a parrot's feather, a snail shell, a bit of string.

"Here it is!" he cried. He held up a straight pin with a coloured bulb on the end. It was big enough to skewer a butterfly – or a fairy – right through the middle.

"Now hold still," Peter said. Gripping the pin in one hand, he reached up to grab Tink and Terence with the other.

"Fly!" Terence screamed to Tink.

Just before Peter's stubby fingers closed around them, the fairies turned and fled towards the exit.

9

BUT AS THEY reached the roots of the jack-fruit tree, they heard a whoop of laughter behind them.

Tink stopped and glanced back over her shoulder. Peter was clutching his stomach and shaking with laughter.

"Oh, Tink!" he gasped. "You should have seen the looks on your faces. Butterflies! Oh, I am funny. Oh, oh." He bent over as another round of laughter seized him.

Terence, who had been just ahead of

Tink, also stopped and turned. Frowning, he came to hover next to her. He had never met Peter Pan face to face before and he was starting to think that he wasn't going to like him very much.

But Tink was smiling. It had only been a joke! Peter *did* remember her!

At last Peter stopped laughing. He bounded up to Tink and Terence, his eyes shining.

"Tink!" he cried. "It's awful great to see you. Where've you been hiding?"

"Hello, Peter," Tink replied. "Meet my friend Terence."

"A boy pixie! Fantastic!" Peter cried, turning to stare at Terence.

The grin on his face was so wide and enthusiastic that Terence's heart softened. The thing was, it was impossible not to like Peter Pan. He had the eagerness of a puppy, the cleverness of a fox and the freedom of a lark – all rolled into one spry, redheaded boy.

"You'll never guess what I've got, Tink. Come and see!" He said it as if Tink had been away for a mere few hours and had now come back to play.

Peter led Tink and Terence over to a corner of the hideout and pulled a wooden cigar box out of a hole in the wall. The word "Tarantula" was burned onto the lid. It was the name of the cigars Captain Hook liked to smoke. Peter had found the empty box on the beach, where Hook had thrown it away.

"I keep my most important things in my treasure chest," Peter explained to Terence, gesturing to the box. "The Lost Boys know better than to go poking around in here."

"Where are the Lost Boys?" Tink asked.

Peter thought for a moment. "They must still be hiding," he replied finally. "We were playing hide-and-seek in the forest yesterday.

But when it was my turn to look, I spotted a bobcat stalking a rabbit. Course, I wanted to see if he caught him, so I followed them. I guess I forgot to go back and look for the boys."

"Do you think they're lost?" Terence asked.

Peter grinned. "Course they're lost! They're the Lost Boys! I'll go find them later." He shrugged, then added, "Anyway, that bobcat never did catch the rabbit."

Peter lifted the lid of the cigar box. "Now . . ." Reaching inside, he took out a small object. He held it out towards Tink and Terence in the palm of his hand. It was yellowish white and shaped like a triangle, with razor-sharp edges that narrowed to a point.

Tink clasped her hands together. "Oh!" she gasped. "You got it!"

"What is it?" Terence asked.

"A shark's tooth," Peter replied, just a bit smugly. "Isn't it swell? I'm going to put it on a string and make a necklace."

"The first time I met Peter, he was trying to steal a shark's tooth," Tink explained to Terence.

"That's right!" exclaimed Peter. "I'd made a bet with the boys that I could steal a tooth from a live shark. I built a small raft out of birchwood and was paddling out to sea . . ."

From the way he began, Terence could tell that Peter had told this story many times before, and that he loved telling it.

"I had just paddled beyond the reef," Peter continued, "when I felt something bump the underside of my raft."

"The shark?" asked Terence.

Peter nodded. "He was looking for his lunch. But he didn't know that I was looking for him, too!"

"How did you plan to get his tooth?" Terence asked.

"I meant to stun him with my oar, then steal the tooth while he was out cold," said Peter. "But he was bigger than I'd thought, and before I knew it, he'd bitten my little raft right in half! I was sinking fast and it looked like the end for me, when suddenly I heard a jingling sound over my head. I looked up and there was Tinker Bell. She yelled down at me . . ."

"'Fly, silly boy!'" Tink and Peter cried together. They laughed, remembering.

"But I didn't know how to fly," Peter told Terence. "So Tink taught me how, right then and there. She sprinkled some fairy dust on me and before I knew it, I'd zipped up into the air, out of the shark's reach. Boy, was he mad!"

"So, you went back and got the shark tooth this time?" Tink asked Peter, pointing to the tooth in his hand.

Peter shrugged. "Naw. A mermaid gave this to me. But now I'm going to go out and get the whole shark!" He pointed to the fishing rod and the wooden hook he'd been carving.

Tink and Peter both burst out laughing.

Terence smiled, watching them. He felt glad that Tink looked so happy. But it also made him sad. What if she decided to stay here in the forest with Peter?

Tink *was* happy. She had discovered that it wasn't so hard to see Peter, after all! She'd only needed a friend to help her find that out. She saw Terence's smile and she smiled back at him.

Just then, Tink caught sight of something in the cigar box. Her eyes widened. "My hammer!" she exclaimed.

"I saved it for you, Tink," Peter said proudly. "I knew you'd be back for it."

Tink reached into the box and picked up the hammer. It fitted perfectly in her hand. She tapped it lightly into the palm of her other hand, then closed her eyes and sighed. She felt as if she'd come home after a long, long trip.

Then, to Terence's joy and relief, Tink turned to Peter and said, "It's been so good to see you, Peter. But we have to go back to the fairy kingdom now."

Peter looked at her in surprise. "What? Now? But what about hide-and-seek?"

Tink shook her head. She was glad to realize that she didn't want to stay, not for hide-and-seek or anything else. She wanted to get back to Pixie Hollow, back to her pots and pans. That was where she belonged.

Tink flew so close to Peter's face that he had to cross his eyes to see her. She kissed the bridge of his freckled nose. "I'll come back soon to visit," she promised. And she meant it.

Then, taking Terence's hand, she flew back out of the jackfruit tree and into the forest.

10

As Tink headed back to the fairy kingdom with Terence, one last thing was bothering her.

She didn't want all of Pixie Hollow to know about the hammer and her trip to see Peter. Enough hurtful gossip had already spread through the kingdom. Tink didn't want any more.

She wanted to ask Terence if he would keep their trip to Peter's a secret between them. But before she could, he turned to her. "I don't think anyone else needs to know about this trip, do you?" he asked. "You've got your hammer back and that's what matters."

Tink grinned and nodded. What a good friend Terence was.

"The only thing is," Terence said, "how will we convince everyone that you have your talent back?"

Tink thought for a moment. "I have an idea," she said.

Putting on a burst of speed, Tink raced Terence all the way back to Pixie Hollow.

When they got to the Home Tree, Tink went straight to Queen Ree's quarters.

One of the queen's attendants opened the door. "Tink, welcome," the attendant said when she saw her.

"I've come to fix the queen's bathtub," Tink told her.

Terence, who was standing behind Tink,

grinned. Tink was clever. This was the perfect way to prove that her talent was back. Terence didn't doubt that Tink could fix the tub. She was the best pots-and-pans fairy in the kingdom.

But the attendant hesitated. Everyone had heard about Tink and her talent. She wanted to refuse to let Tink fix it.

Just then, Ree stepped forwards. She had heard Tink's request. "Come in, Tink," she said.

"I've come to fix your bathtub," Tink repeated to the queen.

Ree looked at Tink. In Tink's blue eyes, she saw a fierce certainty that hadn't been there the day before, when they'd talked in the gazebo.

Ree nodded. "Take Tink to the bathtub," she told her attendant.

The attendant looked startled, but she

turned and began to lead Tink away.

Just before Tink left, Terence grabbed her hand. "Good luck," he said.

Tink held up her hammer and gave his hand a squeeze. "I don't need it!" she said.

Have you ever wondered what makes a flower **grOW** or why a firefly has such a magical **glow**? It's all the work of the fairies!

Would you like to learn more about Tinker Bell and her fairy friends?

Read on to answer all of your questions about the fairies of **Pixie Hollow** and their amazing, *magical* talents!

Step into the enchanting world of Pixie Hollow where believing is just the beginning!

Born of a baby's first laugh, fairies make
their home deep in the magical heart of Never
Land…in the enchanting **Pixie Hollow**. Magic
and the sparkle of fairy dust fills the air, and
the sounds of cheeky fairy laughter can be
heard everywhere you go!

As soon as a fairy arrives in **Pixie Hollow** she'll
find out what her special talent is.

Just like human children, every fairy is
different and special. Some can create fire with
a snap of their fairies' fingers, others can fly
faster than any bird – some fairies can even talk
to the birds in their own language!

Pots and Kettles Fairies

If you ever go to **Pixie Hollow**, you'll find **Tinker Bell**
hard at work in her teakettle workshop with
her tinker's hammer in her hand. She'll always greet
you with a warm smile, a friendly joke and an
adventure to embark upon!

This sassy pixie's special talent is the ability to fix
things. Give **Tink** anything that's broken and she'll
mend it in a moment!

Fixing fairies, like **Tink**, love a challenge and
anything that looks as though it will be
tough to repair will be by far their
favourite thing to fix.

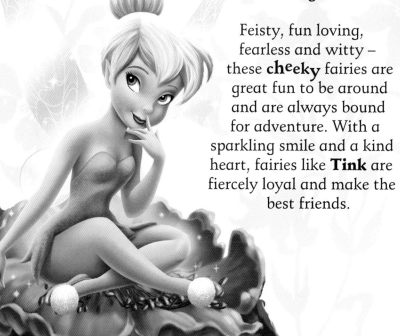

Feisty, fun loving,
fearless and witty –
these **cheeky** fairies are
great fun to be around
and are always bound
for adventure. With a
sparkling smile and a kind
heart, fairies like **Tink** are
fiercely loyal and make the
best friends.

Water Fairies

Water-talent fairies are simply amazing creatures! They have a magical control over water and can bend it into any shape or form. Water fairies could turn a murky puddle into a glistening fountain or a simple water droplet into a whirling water spiral.

These fairies are easy going and tend to go with the flow of things. **Water fairies** have a **calming and gentle** influence on other fairies. They're as refreshing as rain, as cool as a stream and as deep and secretive as the ocean!

Water fairies are generous and very emotional – they cry easily and have to keep lots of leafkerchiefs nearby!

Garden Fairies

Some fairies prefer to walk through Never Land instead of flying. These fairies are **garden-talent fairies**; they love to feel the soft grass between their tiny toes!

These green-fingered pixies have a special power over plants and flowers. Garden fairies can make any seed **grOW** and any bud **bloom.**

Besides having the best gardens in **Pixie Hollow**, garden fairies can sense how plants feel and will be the first to know if a flower is happy, sad or scared. They're quick witted and full of charm!

Animal Fairies

Animal fairies possess the amazing ability to talk to animals in their own language – they can speak bird, caterpillar, squirrel, butterfly and many other languages. They can also read the thoughts and feelings of any animal.

Animal fairies are full of mischief and love to play with their furry friends. These fairies make great friends, as they're always ready for fun and love playing all sorts of magical games. However, many animal fairies get on better with animals than they do with other fairies so getting to know them can be difficult.

Light Fairies

Light-talent fairies shine as brightly as the sun and can light up anything with their beautiful **glow**. These special fairies can shape, bend and even create light with nothing but a wave of their hand. You'd never need a torch again with one of these fairies around - with a snap of their fingers, sparks of light fly into the sky and magically illuminate the world around them.

Just like their talents, these fairies are **fiery** and **feisty!** They always speak their mind and are honest about everything. **Light-talent fairies** always look on the bright side of things; they have naturally sunny dispositions and can cheer up anyone!

Take the Fairy Talent Test!

**If you were a fairy, which talent would you have?
Take the test below to find out.**

1. What is your favourite hobby?
A. Swimming
B. Gardening
C. Fixing things
D. Playing with your pets
E. Playing outside in the sunshine

2. What is your favourite animal?
A. A dolphin
B. You prefer flowers to animals
C. A dog
D. You can't pick because you love all animals
E. A firefly

3. What is your favourite colour?
A. Blue
B. Green
C. Copper
D. Earth red
E. Yellow

4. Your favourite outfit would be...
A. A swimsuit
B. Anything worn with Wellington boots!
C. Jeans and a t-shirt
D. A woolly jumper
E. A colourful dress

5. What word describes you best?
A. Calm
B. Witty
C. Adventurous
D. Playful
E. Fiery

6. Where is your favourite place to be?
A. By the ocean
B. In your garden
C. Anywhere you can find things to fix
D. Anywhere you can be with animals
E. In the sun

Answers:
- *If you scored mostly As then you'd be a water fairy.*
- *If you scored mostly Bs then you'd be a garden fairy.*
- *If you scored mostly Cs then you'd be a pots and kettles fairy.*
- *If you scored mostly Ds then you'd be a animal fairy.*
- *If you scored mostly Es then you'd be a light fairy.*

Lily's Pesky Plant

WRITTEN BY
KIRSTEN LARSEN

ILLUSTRATED BY
JUDITH HOLMES CLARKE
& THE DISNEY STORYBOOK ARTISTS

1

EARLY ONE MORNING, Lily woke to the sound of birds chirping in the topmost branches of the Home Tree, the ancient maple where Never Land's fairies live. Opening her eyes, she saw the walls of her room stretch ever so slightly as the great tree reached its branches towards the early-morning sun. Lily pushed back her fern-frond quilt and yawned, stretching her arms up into the air.

Lily climbed out of bed and opened the doors of her wardrobe, which was made from a dried gourd. She chose a thistledown shirt and knickers woven from dandelion fluff. Unlike some fairies, Lily didn't like spider-silk gowns and shoes with heels as thin as pine needles. She liked simple, sturdy clothes.

In the tearoom, Lily had her usual breakfast, a cup of lemongrass tea and a slice of poppy seed cake. Some of the other garden-talent fairies at Lily's table sat for a while at breakfast. They refilled their pots of tea and spread heaps of black cherry jam on their bread. But not Lily. The moment her plate and cup were empty, she pushed them aside and flew off to her garden.

Lily's garden was just two frog's leaps beyond the Home Tree, right in the heart of Pixie Hollow. All the fairies agreed that it was one of the nicest places in the entire fairy kingdom. On one side of her garden was a hedge of raspberry bushes. On the other side, a wild rosebush sweetly scented the air. Everywhere bright red and orange poppies sprang from the ground. Clusters of Queen Anne's lace and lilac made pleasant groves where a fairy could sit and think. And throughout the garden, sweet clover sprouted in fairy-sized beds. They were perfect for taking naps in.

The garden was a favourite spot of many fairies, who were always dropping by. Harvest-talent fairies picked raspberries from the bushes. Healing-talent fairies collected herbs for their potions. Other fairies simply liked to walk among the beautiful flowers.

Lily welcomed them all. Next to working in her garden, Lily's favourite thing was watching fairies enjoy the beautiful plants she grew. The fairies also enjoyed Lily's company. With her friendly, direct smile and her sparkling dark eyes, she was as fresh and lovely as the flowers she grew.

As soon as Lily got to her garden, she called out, "Bumble!" At once, a large bee zipped out of the flowers and flew up to her. Bumble was yellow, round and fuzzy all over. He wasn't Lily's pet, exactly. He had just showed up one day and never left. The two had become good friends.

Bumble always followed Lily as she took care of her plants. She watered them. She checked their leaves for spots. That morning Lily saw that some of the daffodils had been toppled by a breeze. She tied the stems to stakes to help them stand sturdy and strong again.

When she was done making the rounds in her garden, Lily lay down on a patch of soft moss to watch the grass grow. To you this might sound boring, but for her it was every bit as exciting as watching butterfly races (a favourite fairy pastime). Lily was certain that the blades of grass grew faster when they knew she was watching.

Unluckily for Lily, she was the only fairy in all of Pixie Hollow to have this hobby. When others saw her lying in the grass, they usually thought she was doing nothing at all. Often, they would start talking to her. This frustrated Lily, for it broke her concentration.

And that was exactly what happened that morning. Bumble was buzzing around the buttercups in the corner of her garden and Lily was lying nearby, watching a (very slow) race between two blades of grass. One blade was winning, and Lily was urging the other one to catch up, when a voice broke through her thoughts.

"I say, what a funny thing!" The voice was loud and a bit shrill.

Lily didn't move, except to lower her eyelids. She hoped whoever it was would think she was sleeping and go away.

"I said, what a funny thing!" the voice cried, even more shrilly.

Lily sighed and opened her eyes. A tall fairy was standing over her. She had curly hair the colour of a wax bean and a long, narrow nose that was red at the tip.

"Hello, Iris," said Lily, sitting up. "What's so funny?"

"Why, just look at your buttercups."

Lily looked. She didn't see anything funny about them.

"They're the biggest I've ever seen!" Iris exclaimed. "You ought to call them butter-*bowls* instead." She chuckled at her own joke.

Lily smiled politely. "They do seem happy," she replied. Lily didn't care how big or small a plant was, as long as it was happy. That was the reason the plants in her garden grew so well – she made sure they were all content.

"Of course, they're nothing like the buttercups I used to grow," Iris went on. "They were as big as soup pots and yellow as the sun. I'll tell you a secret I learned from a Tiffen: you have to give them *real butter*."

Lily raised her eyebrows in surprise. The Tiffens were big-eared creatures who grew bananas. Their farms weren't far from Pixie Hollow. Lily had never heard of a Tiffen who grew buttercups.

Then again, she thought, *what do I know about Tiffens?* Lily didn't spend very much time outside her garden.

Iris gave her a smug little nod. Like Lily, Iris was a garden-talent fairy. She had once had her own garden, but it was so long ago no one could remember what it had been like.

Then Iris had begun writing her plant book. Now, she claimed, she was much too busy to do any real gardening. Instead, she went around poking her nose into other fairies' gardens. She said she was collecting information for her book. But she usually did more talking than listening.

Lily couldn't imagine what it would be like to be a garden fairy without a garden. She thought it must be awful.

Iris plopped down on a spotted red toadstool and flipped open the birch-bark cover of her book. She turned its pages, which were made from leaves. Iris carried the book with her everywhere she went.

"Anyway, Lily," Iris said, "I've come because I'm worried about your snapdragons. Now, don't get me wrong. They seem perfectly healthy and strong. But when I went to take a peek at their petals the other day, one snapped at me!"

"They're *snap*dragons, Iris," Lily pointed out patiently. "It's their nature to be cranky."

"Well, I *know* a thing or two about snapdragons, Lily," Iris said. "And you can't just

let them act wild. You've got to *train* them."
Iris continued to flip through the pages of her
book. "I found a perfectly brilliant way to keep
them from snapping." She tapped the page
she'd opened to. "Here, I'll read it to you. 'A
Cure for Snappish Snapdragons, by Iris. If your
snapdragons have bad manners, you must pinch
their leaves whenever they snap at you. . . .'"

As Iris read on, Lily's toes began to wig-
gle impatiently. Suddenly, she blurted out,
"Actually, Iris, I was just about to leave."

It wasn't true, and Lily wasn't quite sure
why she'd said it. She knew Iris only meant to
be helpful. But maybe she was annoyed with
Iris for interrupting her peaceful morning.
Or maybe it was just that Lily *liked* her snapdragons to be snappish. Whatever the reason,
on this particular day, Lily just didn't feel like
listening to Iris.

"Where are you going? I could come with

you and tell you more on the way," Iris offered.

"Oh, but . . . I'm going fern spotting. Possum ferns, that is," Lily said quickly. Any fairy knew it was impossible to look for possum ferns and talk at the same time. The ferns were shy and would wilt completely if they heard a noise.

"Oh. Okay, then. Another time." Iris blew her nose into a leaf kerchief. She looked disappointed, and Lily felt a little pang. She wished she hadn't lied about going to the forest. But it was too late to take it back now.

"Yes, another time. See you, Iris," Lily said. She rose into the air and flew off into the forest.

When she was just out of sight from the garden, Lily landed near the roots of an old oak tree.

"I'll just go for a short walk," she told herself as she set out along a narrow path through the bushes. "Then I'll go back." She figured Iris would have moved to someone else's garden by then.

Most fairies never went to the forest alone because of snakes, owls, and hawks. And fairies almost never walked unless their wings were too wet to fly. But Lily was brave, and what was more, she liked walking. She felt closer to the plants when her feet were on the ground.

Lily walked along the forest floor. She kept an eye out for snakes. High above, the wind rustled the leaves of the trees. Lily took off her shoes. She liked the feeling of the damp soil between her toes.

Just then, she spotted something curled against the base of a rock. It was a silvery green plant with tightly coiled, velvety leaves. Lily smiled.

"A possum fern!" she whispered. She had spotted one after all! Holding her breath, Lily silently crept towards the rare plant to get a closer look.

Suddenly, something crashed through the leaves over her head. Lily gasped and flew for cover between the roots of a nearby tree. Had a hawk just swooped at her? Trembling, she peered out from behind the root and scanned the forest.

But there was no sign of a hawk. The forest was still and quiet. Lily looked over at the possum fern and saw that its leaves had uncoiled and turned brown. It had heard the noise and was playing dead.

Then Lily saw something that made her gasp again. In the spot where she had just been standing lay a strange seed.

2

AT LEAST, LILY thought it was a seed. It was
hard to say for sure. She had never seen anything quite like it before.

It was as big as a chestnut and a pearly
white colour, like the inside of an oyster shell.
The ends tapered into points. A few fibres
stuck out like hairs from the tips.

As soon as her heart stopped racing, Lily
flew over and landed next to the strange object.
She picked up a twig and poked it. Nothing
happened.

Lily felt braver. She touched it with her fingertips. The surface felt cool and smooth, like a sea-polished rock.

Now Lily was sure it was a seed. Her gardening instincts told her there was life inside it – the sleeping life of a plant waiting to grow.

"But where did it come from?" Lily asked aloud.

Just then, she heard a loud chittering sound above her. She looked up. A squirrel was chattering at her from a branch overhead.

Lily laughed. Now she knew where the seed had come from. The squirrel probably wasn't used to seeing fairies walking on the ground. It had dropped the seed in surprise.

"Don't worry," she called to the squirrel. "I'm leaving soon!" The squirrel chattered at her again, then darted away along a tree branch.

Lily looked back down at the seed. *What is it?* she wondered. For once, she wished she were an animal-talent fairy. Then she could talk to the squirrel and ask him where the mysterious seed had come from.

"What kind of plant are you?" Lily whispered to the seed. As she said the words, something occurred to her, and her eyes widened. "That's it!" she exclaimed. "I'll plant it! After all, the only way to find out what a seed will become is to watch it grow."

Lily reached down to pick it up. To her surprise, it was heavy. She sprinkled a pinch of fairy dust over the seed. It grew lighter in her arms.

Clutching her treasure against her chest, Lily rose into the air and flew in the direction of her garden.

Back at her garden, Lily found Iris still sitting on the toadstool, right where she had left her.

"Oh, Lily, you're back already," said Iris. "Did you get to see some possum ferns? The last time I went possum fern spotting, I saw exactly three dozen of them. Although for some reason, they all were playing dead. . . ."

"I found something even better," Lily told Iris. She no longer felt annoyed with her. She was much too excited about her find. Gently Lily placed the big seed on the ground.

Iris was so surprised, she sneezed three times in a row. "What an amazing seed!" she cried, after she'd blown her nose. "Whatever is it?"

"You don't know?" Lily asked. "I was hoping you would. I found it in the forest just now. I've never seen one before."

Bumble heard Lily's voice and flew over to greet her. Lily patted his fuzzy side.

"What do you think of my new seed, Bumble?" she asked.

The bee landed on the seed, paused for a moment, then flew off in the direction of the roses. Bumble was more interested in flowers than seeds.

Iris squinted closely at the seed. Then she pulled out her writing splinter and made a note in her book. She began to draw a picture of the seed next to it.

"Hi, Lily. Hi, Iris. What is that? It's so lovely!" said a friendly voice. Rani, a pretty water-talent fairy with long, blonde hair, walked over to them.

"Hi, Rani," said Lily. "It's some kind of seed. We're not sure what. I found it today in the –"

"– beach cove?" Rani asked. She had a habit of finishing others' sentences.

"No, the forest," said Lily.

"Oh. It's just that it reminds me of a shell," Rani said fondly. She squatted down to admire the seed.

"I'll bet that's it," Iris said. She tapped her writing splinter thoughtfully against her cheek. "I'll bet it's a seaweed seed." She made another note in her book.

Lily shrugged. She had no idea what a seaweed seed looked like, or whether there was such a thing. Fairies never went underwater. Their wings would soak up too much water and drag them down.

But Rani shook her head. "No, I don't think so," she said. "I've never seen anything like it before."

Iris frowned. Lily knew Iris didn't like to be wrong. But she couldn't argue with Rani. The water-talent fairy had visited the mermaids in order to help save Never Land, and she had even cut off her wings to do it. She was the only fairy in Never Land who had ever been underwater. On the subject of seaweed seeds, she certainly knew more than anyone in Pixie Hollow.

Scowling, Iris crossed out what she had just written.

"Well," said Lily, "there's only one way to find out what it is." She picked up a shovel and drove the tip into the ground.

Iris looked up from her book. "You're going to plant it? Just like that?" she asked. She sounded alarmed. "But you don't know how much sunlight it needs. Or how much water. And what if it doesn't get along with the other flowers? And . . . and . . ."

Lily smiled. Iris certainly knew a lot about plants. *But knowing about plants isn't all there is to gardening*, Lily thought. *Sometimes you just have to trust your instincts.*

"I'm sure everything will be fine," she said.

3

"What is that sound?" Lily exclaimed.

It was a few days after she had planted the seed. Lily had been wrapping spider silk around some violets that had caught a chill when she was interrupted by a terrible racket. It sounded like big metal teeth chomping together.

Chomp! Chomp! Chomp!

Lily cupped her hands over her ears. The sound was coming from the other side of her garden. She hurried towards it.

Suddenly, Lily stopped short in surprise. There was Iris, sitting atop a strange contraption.

It had a seat and pedals. At the front of the machine was a set of huge metal jaws. As Lily watched, Iris dumped a bucket of kitchen rubbish into the jaws. Then she put her feet on the pedals. As her legs moved, the metal jaws chewed up the rubbish.

Chomp! Chomp! Chomp!

"Just making a little food for our seed!" Iris shouted over the noise. She stopped pedalling and held up a bucket for Lily to see. It was full of mulched vegetable scraps.

"It's chock-full of nutrients for a growing plant." Iris beamed proudly.

Bumble flew around Lily in dizzy circles. He hated loud noises.

"Well, that's . . . very thoughtful, Iris," said Lily. She eyed the machine uncertainly.

"Only the best for our little plant," Iris said. She went back to pedalling. Lily winced and put her hands over her ears.

Ever since Lily had planted the mysterious seed, Iris had come to her garden every day to check on it. And each time, she had some new idea for how to make the plant grow faster.

One day Iris had turned up with a daisy umbrella, insisting that the seed would grow best in the shade. The next day she fretted that it wasn't getting the sunlight it needed. In the afternoons, Iris would sit on the spotted toadstool, talking about the seed and writing in her book.

"It's not every day that someone finds a new plant," Iris told Lily. "I'm writing everything down. You know, for future garden fairies."

Lily just smiled. Iris was the only garden fairy she knew who liked to read about gardening. The other fairies just *gardened*. Still, she couldn't blame Iris for being excited. Lily was just as curious to see what kind of plant would grow.

Iris finally finished mulching the rubbish. She picked up the bucket of plant food and set off in the direction of the seed. Lily went back to tending her violets.

Suddenly, Iris shrieked.

Lily dropped the spider silk and raced back to the toadstool. Maybe Iris had hurt herself! But the red-nosed fairy was grinning from ear to ear. "Look, Lily!" she said breathlessly. "It's sprouted!"

Lily looked where Iris was pointing. Sure enough, a small seedling was growing where they'd planted the mysterious seed.

Lily clapped her hands together. "Oh, it's beautiful," she whispered.

In fact, the seedling wasn't beautiful at all.

Its leaves were a sickly yellow colour. Its stem was covered with little spots, as if it had a bad case of chicken pox. But that was the thing about Lily. She thought every plant was beautiful.

Iris was thrilled. "Vidia!" she called out to a fairy passing by. "Come look at our new little plant!"

Vidia flew over to them. She looked at the seedling and made a face. "Darlings, I've never seen anything so ugly in my life," she declared.

Iris's face fell. Lily frowned. *Trust Vidia to say something mean*, she thought. The dark-haired, fast-flying fairy was as spiteful as they came.

"It reminds me of a sick caterpillar I saw once," Vidia went on. "If I were you, I'd put it out of its misery now. Iris, dear, why don't you run along and get a shovel to dig it up?"

Iris's glow flared with anger. She scowled at Vidia.

Lily ignored Vidia. "Iris, let's give it water," she said. "It looks like it could use some."

Iris gave Vidia one last angry glance. Then she picked up a bucket and hurried off to the stream.

"Lily, dear, how can you stand having her around all the time?" Vidia said. She glanced at Iris's back. "A garden fairy without a garden." She shook her head. "*Tsk, tsk.* How sad." But Vidia didn't sound sad. She sounded amused.

"She's better company than *some* fairies," Lily replied.

Vidia gave her a sugary smile. "I can take a hint, sweetie," she said. "Have fun with your little sprout. But you should watch out for those spots. They look contagious."

Rising into the air, Vidia put on a burst of speed and disappeared.

For the next few days, Lily and Iris carefully tended the plant. They watered it every morning. They talked to it every afternoon. The seedling seemed to enjoy the attention. It grew amazingly fast. Soon it towered over the fairies' heads.

It grew uglier, too. The small spots grew into big warts. Sticky sap dripped from its bark. It sprouted thin, droopy branches Sometimes Lily thought Vidia was right. I *did* look a bit like a sick caterpillar – a great big sick caterpillar with droopy legs.

Lily didn't care. She could tell that the plant was happy, so she was happy, too.

The other fairies weren't quite so open-minded. "Lily, come quick!" Tinker Bell burst into the tearoom one morning. "I just flew past your garden. A monster is attacking your buttercups!"

Lily dropped her teacup and the two fairies raced out of the Home Tree.

Outside Lily's garden, they paused behind the rosebush. With silent looks they agreed they would take the beast by surprise. Tinker Bell drew her dagger. The two fairies crept forwards.

"There it is!" Tink whispered, pointing.

Lily began to laugh. She laughed until tears rolled down her cheeks.

Tink stared at her in surprise.

At last Lily flew over and landed beside the "monster." "Tink," she said between chuckles, "meet my newest plant."

"That's a *plant?*" Tink said. She blushed and lowered her dagger. Taking a few steps forwards, she peered up at its ugly branches. "What kind is it?"

"I don't know. I found the seed in the forest and planted it," Lily explained.

"Well, it's very interesting," replied

Tink. "But I'd hate to bump into it on a dark night."

Even the other garden fairies were doubtful. "I've never seen anything like it," said Rosetta. "Are you sure you want such an ugly plant in your garden?"

"I'm sure," said Lily.

The other fairies looked around at the beautiful flowers and shook their heads. But they didn't say anything more. If nothing else, they thought, the mysterious plant kept Iris away from *their* gardens.

4

ONE MORNING, LILY noticed a strange odour in her garden. It smelled like rotten tomatoes, and a little bit like sour milk.

How odd, Lily thought. She began to walk through her garden, looking for the source of the stink.

Soon she came to the red spotted toadstool. It was empty. Iris hadn't yet arrived.

Lily covered her nose with her hands. The smell was even stronger here.

Bumble, who had followed her, began

to flit around nervously. Suddenly, he darted away.

"I wonder what's got into him?" Lily said to herself.

She turned and saw something that made her forget all about Bumble. The mysterious plant had grown flowers. And what strange flowers! They practically exploded from its branches. The centres of the giant flowers were pale and sticky-looking. Spiky white petals stuck out from the edges, like crazy uncombed hair.

The flowers were not pretty. But in their own way they were interesting, Lily thought.

Curious, she rose into the air until she was face to face with one of the flowers. She leaned forwards, closed her eyes, and . . .

Ugh! Lily's eyes flew open. Her wings froze in mid-flutter. She dropped out of the air and landed on the ground with a painful thud.

The horrible rotten-tomato smell was coming from the flowers.

Bzzzzzzzzzzzzzz!

Bumble zipped over to Lily to see if she was okay. A moment later he darted away again. He couldn't stand the flowers' smell.

"Lily, are you all right?" asked a muffled voice.

Lily looked up and saw Iris hurrying over to her. She was holding a leafkerchief over her nose and mouth. "I saw you fall," she told Lily.

"I'm all right," Lily replied. She rubbed a bruised spot on her knee. "Just surprised. I really wasn't expecting it to . . . *stink* so much!"

Iris held out a clean leaf kerchief. Lily took it gratefully. Covering their noses, the two fairies stared up at the big, smelly flowers. Iris looked worried.

"You've gone and spoiled it," Iris complained. "That's what happens when you baby plants. They develop obnoxious personalities."

Behind her leafkerchief, Lily smiled. Iris had babied the plant even more than Lily had.

But Lily didn't think that was the problem. In fact, she didn't think there was any problem. She had a feeling that the plant was doing exactly what it was supposed to do.

Before she could say so, other voices interrupted.

"What *is* that smell?"

"It's as if all the food in the kitchen went bad!"

"It's coming from over there!"

A little group of fairies and sparrow men came flying towards them from the Home Tree. They were all wearing clothes pegs on their noses. They came to a sudden stop when they saw the giant flowers.

"Goodness!"

"How ugly!"

"*That's* what smells so bad."

"Lily, what in the name of Never Land is wrong with that plant?" asked Dulcie, a baking-talent fairy. Her voice sounded funny because of the clothes peg pinching her nose.

"Nothing," replied Lily. "I don't think there's anything wrong with it."

"Well, can you do something about that smell? It's blowing in the windows of the tea-room," said a serving-talent sparrow man. "Queen Ree sent us to find out where it was coming from." Ree was the fairies' nickname for Queen Clarion.

Lily looked around. Her eyes fell on a patch of lavender.

"I have an idea," she said. Hurrying over to her lavender, she picked a few pieces. She tucked a bit inside her leaf kerchief and tied it around her nose and mouth like a mask. The lavender's sweetness covered up the bad smell.

She handed the rest of the lavender to the other fairies. They pinned the flowers to their noses with the clothes pegs. Then Lily returned to the lavender bush and began filling her arms with flowers.

"Everyone come and pick some," she instructed. "We can take it back to the other fairies in the Home Tree."

Just then, she heard a sound.

BZZZZZZZZZZZZZZZZZ . . .

At first Lily thought Bumble had got his head stuck in a flower (it happened sometimes) and was buzzing for help. But the sound grew louder.

BZZZZZZZZZZZZZZZZZ . . .

She looked up. A black cloud seemed to

be moving towards them across the sky.

BZZZZZZZZZZZZZZZ . . .

Lily looked closer. It wasn't a cloud at all. It was a huge swarm of wasps!

"Look out!" Lily cried.

The fairies leaped into the lavender for cover as the wasps dived towards them. Nearby, Bumble hid in a patch of clover.

But the wasps weren't after the fairies. Buzzing loudly, they clustered around the flowers on the mysterious plant. They seemed to like the strange, stinky smell.

In the lavender, the fairies waited . . . and waited and waited. They hoped the wasps would get tired of the flowers and go away.

But the swarm only grew.

Lily's legs began to feel cramped from crouching so long.

"What do we do now?" Dulcie whispered to Lily.

Lily sighed. She had no idea what to do. They couldn't make a dash for the Home Tree because they might get stung. A single sting could be fatal to a fairy – after all, the wasps were nearly as big as their heads. But they couldn't hide in the lavender forever.

Just then, Lily heard a caw. She peeped out of the lavender and saw a large black shape swoop down from the sky. Another dark shape followed right behind it.

Ravens!

And riding on the ravens' backs, right between their wings, were fairies.

5

THE RAVENS DIVED at the wasps. They flapped their wings and cawed fiercely. The swarm began to break up. The wasps were afraid of the huge black birds.

Finally, the last wasp was gone. Lily and the other fairies climbed out of the lavender.

The ravens landed next to them. On their backs were Beck and Fawn, two animal-talent fairies.

"A scout saw the swarm go into your garden," Beck explained. "We thought there might be trouble. So we called the ravens."

Beck said something to the ravens that Lily couldn't understand. Then she and Fawn fluttered to the ground. With a great rustle of feathers, the birds stretched their enormous wings and flew away.

"Is anyone hurt?" asked Fawn.

Iris, who had been silent, suddenly burst into tears. "I nearly got stung!" she cried. "A wasp came this close to me!" She held her hands an inch apart.

Some of the fairies from the kitchen frowned. After all, everyone had been in danger. Yet Iris seemed concerned only about herself.

Fawn gently patted Iris's back to calm her down. She was used to taking care of frightened animals. Frightened fairies weren't that different.

"Anyone else?" asked Beck.

The other fairies and sparrow men shook their heads. They were all scared, but no one had been harmed.

"Come on, Iris," Beck said. "Let's go back to the Home Tree. A cup of tea with honey will make you feel better."

"And in the meantime, someone ought to do something about that plant," Fawn added.

"What do you mean 'do something'?" Lily asked.

"Well, chop it down or pull it up. You know, get rid of it," Fawn said.

Lily drew back as if she'd been slapped. Chop down a plant? Just hearing the words made her legs ache. She had never chopped down a plant in her life. She couldn't even pull weeds from her garden – instead, she encouraged them to grow elsewhere.

"The wasps liked those flowers," Fawn explained. "They could come back at any moment."

Lily looked at Iris. She hoped Iris would say something good about the plant. After all, Iris loved it as much as Lily did.

Iris's eyes were wide and her face was pale. But she didn't say anything.

Lily turned back to Beck and Fawn. "The plant is growing in my garden," she said. "I will take responsibility for it." She looked at Dulcie and the other fairies from the kitchen. "Tell the others in the tearoom. You have my word that no one will be endangered here again."

There was a long pause. "All right," Dulcie said at last. "I'll tell the queen you'll take care of the smell."

The little band of fairies headed back to the Home Tree.

As Beck led her away, Iris glanced back at Lily. Lily thought she looked sorry. But she couldn't say for sure.

For the next few days, Lily was very busy. Every morning she picked armloads of lavender to hand out to the fairies of Pixie Hollow. Her leafkerchief masks were a good way to cover up the smell of the stinky flowers. But it took a lot of lavender to keep everyone happy. Lily's lavender plants were starting to look bare. What would happen when she ran out?

She also worried that the wasps would come back. Every day, she searched the sky for signs of a buzzing black cloud. But the sky remained blue. The only clouds she saw were fluffy and white.

Then one morning, Lily woke with a stuffy nose. Her eyes watered and her throat itched. Her whole head felt as if it were filled with cotton.

"What a terrible time to catch a cold," Lily

said as she climbed out of bed. She dressed slowly. She was already thinking of the work that lay ahead of her. She had to hand out more lavender, and she was behind with her gardening.

When she got to the tearoom, Lily noticed something strange. None of the fairies had on a leafkerchief mask. Instead, they were using their leafkerchiefs to blow their noses. Everyone in the Home Tree seemed to be sick.

"Hi, Lily," the other garden fairies said as she sat down at their table. Lily looked around. All the fairies had watery eyes and runny noses. Some had dandelion-fluff scarves wrapped around their throats. Only Iris looked the same as usual – maybe because she always looked as if she had a cold.

"What an awful cold everyone's got," Lily remarked as she filled her teacup.

"Oh, it's no cold," Rosetta replied stuffily. She dabbed at her nose with a rose petal.

"It's that pink dust."

"Pink dust?" asked Lily.

Rosetta nodded. "It's everywhere. The cleaning-talent fairies can't get rid of it. It makes them sneeze so much, they can't get any work done."

A bleary-eyed serving-talent fairy came to the table to serve their tea. All the teacups were covered with a strange, sticky pink dust.

Suddenly, Lily had a bad feeling. "I'll be right back," she said. She hurried off to her garden.

Sure enough, her entire garden looked as if it had been covered in pink snow. When a slight breeze blew, more pink dust floated down from the flowers on the mysterious plant.

It wasn't dust, Lily realized. It was pollen. And everyone in Pixie Hollow was allergic to it!

6

By the afternoon, pink pollen had covered Pixie Hollow. It floated in the fairies' chestnut soup at lunch. It stuck in their hair. It gummed up their wings. And, of course, it made everyone sneeze.

Iris made *tsk-tsk* noises from her spot on the toadstool. "I told you not to plant that seed without knowing anything about it," she said. She sneezed twice and blew her nose, then looked thoughtfully at the plant. "Still," she added, "it *is* a most extraordinary plant."

Lily frowned at her, but Iris didn't notice. She had already gone back to scribbling in her book.

Just then, a fairy bolted into the garden. She screeched to a stop right in front of Lily. It was Vidia. And she looked furious.

"You should have uprooted that . . . that *thing* when it was a sprout," Vidia snarled. As she spoke, she tried to shake the sticky pollen from her wings. Vidia despised anything that kept her from flying fast. She was so angry, she hadn't even bothered to call Lily dear or darling.

"Here, let me wash your wings, Vidia," Lily said. It was a special kindness to offer to wash another fairy's wings. Lily felt sorry that Vidia was so upset, and it was her way of saying so.

"*I'm* the only fairy who touches my wings," Vidia snapped. She turned and pointed at the tree. "If *you* won't cut it down, I *will*. I'm sure one of the carpenter-talent fairies would be happy to loan me an axe."

And for what might have been the first time in the history of Pixie Hollow, many of the fairies agreed with Vidia. All afternoon, fairies came to Lily to complain about the plant.

"*Ah-choo!* I've had to throw out three acorn puffs," Dulcie told Lily. "Every time I . . . I . . . I – *ah-choo!* – sneeze, the puffs collapse! If there's nothing to eat at dinner tonight, you can blame that plant of yours."

Even Terence, a normally cheerful dust-talent sparrow man, was troubled. "That pink stuff has got mixed in with the fairy dust," he told Lily. "It's messing up everyone's magic. The music-talent fairies' instruments will only play in the key of B minor. And the laundry fairies haven't been able to do the wash. Their soap went haywire and the washroom is eight inches deep in bubbles! Before you know it," he added grimly, "we won't even be able to fly."

Later, Lily found a quiet patch of clover and sat down alone. All day, not a single fairy had come to smell the roses or walk among the flowers of her garden. They had come only to complain.

Bumble saw Lily's slumped shoulders and sad expression. He flew over to her and gently bumped her arm.

When Lily didn't respond, Bumble flew in crazy loops and zigzags. He was pretending he'd had too much pollen. Usually that made Lily laugh.

But Lily didn't even smile. "Not now, Bumble," she said with a sigh.

Lily saw Iris flying towards her. Lily wished she would go away. She didn't need to hear another "I told you so."

"What a day, huh?" Iris said as she landed

in front of Lily.

Lily shrugged.

"Look on the bright side, Lily," Iris said. She sat down beside her in the clover. "Everyone's nose is so stuffed up, no one can *smell* those stinky flowers anymore."

Lily laughed. But a second later her smile faded.

"All the other fairies want me to fix the plant," she told Iris. "But what can I do? Can you stop the clouds from raining? Can you stop the wind from blowing? The plant is just doing what it normally does."

She glanced over at the plant. Despite its ugliness, awful smell, and itchy pollen, there was something special about it.

"The thing is," Lily added, "I think there's more to it than just what we've seen."

Iris nodded. "I feel the same way." A look of alarm crossed her face as another thought occurred to her. "Do you think it could be something bad?" she asked. "After all, it's already caused so much trouble. . . ."

Lily shook her head. "I don't think so. I always know when there's real trouble, because the plants in my garden tell me," she explained. "When they're tense, I know a big storm is coming. If there's a fire anywhere in the forest, my flowers let me know even before I can smell smoke. But since I planted that strange seed in my garden, the other plants seem as happy and healthy as ever."

Iris looked around. It was true. The garden was bursting with colour. Even the leaves of the clover they were sitting in seemed greener and fuller than usual.

"If the plant were really bad, my garden wouldn't look so good." Lily sighed. "But all the other fairies are so angry with me. I don't know what to do. I want the plants in my garden to make other fairies happy, not miser-able."

"They make me happy," Iris said quietly. She looked down and plucked at a cloverleaf. Then she said, "I should have stood up for our plant that day when the wasps came. It was wrong that I didn't."

Lily looked at her and knew that she meant it.

"It's okay," she said.

"I like gardening with you," Iris went on. "None of the other garden fairies like to have me in their gardens. I know what they say behind my back, you know. They say I'm incomplete."

Lily swallowed hard. Before fairies became fairies, they were laughs. But sometimes a bit of laugh broke off and the fairy ended up with something missing. A fairy like that was called "incomplete."

Lily had heard other garden fairies say that about Iris. She hadn't realized that Iris had heard it as well. Suddenly, she felt sorry about the times when she'd wished Iris would go away.

"You're not incomplete," Lily told her.

"Maybe I am," Iris said. "I love plants as much as any garden fairy. But growing them doesn't come naturally to me the way it does to you. You know, I fibbed about the buttercups in my garden. They weren't as big as soup pots. In fact, they weren't very big at all."

Lily looked surprised. Iris had always made a big deal about her garden.

Iris nodded, ashamed. "I could never keep things straight in my head. Which plants need shade, which like more sun. Which plants like to be watered in the morning, and which like water at night. That's why I started to write things down. Then I got carried away. I started to write down everything I'd ever heard about all the plants in Never Land." She shook her head. "But I guess it's not the same as having a garden."

Lily thought about this for a moment. Then she smiled. "You do have a garden," she said.

Iris looked confused.

"Right here." Lily tapped the cover of Iris's plant book. "Your garden is on these pages. I'll bet it has more plants than any garden in Pixie Hollow."

Now Iris smiled. For a while, the two fairies sat quietly with their arms hooked around their knees. They looked up at the strange, ugly plant.

"There *is* something special about that plant," Iris said at last.

"What is that?" asked Lily.

"It made us friends," Iris replied.

That night after dinner, Lily went once more to her garden. She stood for a long time looking at the mysterious plant.

"Where did you come from?" she murmured. "What are you? Why are you causing so many problems?"

A breeze blew. A few more grains of pollen drifted down from the flower. Lily sneezed three times in a row. *Ah-choo! Ah-choo! Ah-choo!*

The wind shifted, and suddenly Lily sensed a change in the garden. The buttercups, the grass, the lavender, even the mysterious plant all seemed alert. It was as if they were waiting for something.

A raindrop fell from the sky. It landed on Lily's head, soaking her hair. More raindrops splashed on the ground around her.

Rain! Around Lily, the plants began to perk up. This was what they had been waiting for.

The rain came down harder. Lily stretched out her arms and let herself get drenched. The rain washed the pink pollen out of her hair and off her skin.

By the time Lily left the garden, her wings were too wet to fly. She had to walk all the way back to the Home Tree. But she didn't mind.

That night, she stayed up late. She watched the rain from the window of her room. For the first time in days, Lily felt happy. The rain was scrubbing Pixie Hollow clean, washing all the pollen away.

7

LILY WOKE WITH A START. Was it morning?
No, her room was still dark. Glancing out her
window, she could see that the sky was starting
to turn grey. It was just before dawn.

Why did I wake up? Lily wondered.

THUMP! Something banged against her
window.

Startled, Lily climbed out of bed. She
crept over to her window and cautiously peered
out.

THUMP! A yellow and black shape threw

itself against the window.

Lily quickly undid the latch. "Bumble!" she cried as the bee flew into the room. "What are you doing here? What's wrong?"

Bumble buzzed urgently around her head. Then Lily heard a faint cry come through the open window.

"HEEEEEELP!"

Someone was in trouble! Without changing out of her nightclothes, Lily raced out of the Home Tree. Bumble followed on her heels.

Outside, she met up with Tinker Bell and Rani. They, too, had heard the cry.

"HEEEEEEELP!"

"It's coming from over there," said Tinker Bell. Tink's hair, which normally she wore in a ponytail, was loose around her shoulders. Both Tink and Rani were still wearing their pyjamas. Like Lily, they had come straight from their beds.

Bumble shot off in the direction Tink had pointed. The fairies followed him. The cries were coming from Lily's garden.

When they got there, they saw Pell and Pluck, two harvest-talent fairies. They were dangling from the branches of the mysterious plant.

Pell and Pluck saw them, too. "Help us!" they cried.

Tink flew over and grabbed Pell's hands. She tried to pull her away from the tree. But Pell's wings seemed to be glued to the branch.

Tink looked closer. "They're stuck in sap!" she cried. "We'll need hot water to unstick them!"

Lily grabbed a watering can and ran over to the little stream. She filled it with water, then brought it to Rani. Rani sprinkled a pinch of fairy dust on the water and waved her hand over it. It began to steam.

Holding the watering can between them, Lily and Tink flew to Pell. Carefully, they poured the hot water over Pell's wings. Slowly, the sap began to loosen. Tink grabbed Pell's wrists.

Snap! Pell's wings came free and she dropped. Only Tink's grip on her wrists kept her from falling. Carefully, Tink lowered her to the ground.

Then Tink and Lily flew to Pluck and freed her wings, too.

When both harvest-talent fairies were on the ground, Lily and Rani used more hot water to wash the rest of the sap from their wings. The sap was hard to scrub away, but luckily neither of the fairies' wings had been hurt.

As Lily and Rani worked, Pell and Pluck talked over one another, explaining what had happened. "We woke up early –" Pell began.

"Like we always do –" Pluck added.

"And came down to the garden to pick raspberries –"

"For breakfast, you know. The cooking fairies were going to make raspberry jam."

"We were flying through the garden –"

"It was still dark out –"

"So we couldn't see anything. And I accidentally bumped against that plant."

"She got stuck!"

"I got stuck! And when Pluck tried to help me, she got stuck, too!"

"And then we heard an owl!"

"We couldn't move."

"We thought he'd catch us for sure!"

"We called and called. We were afraid no one would ever hear us."

"It was so scary."

Pell and Pluck stretched out their wet wings to dry. By now the sun was up. Still, they were shivering in the cool morning air.

"Rani," said Lily, "will you go back to the Home Tree and get some hot tea and –"

"– blankets?" Rani nodded. She put her fingers to her lips and whistled for Brother Dove, who acted as Rani's wings. When he came, Rani climbed on his back and they flew off.

Tink looked at Lily. "The other fairies are going to be upset," she said.

Lily nodded. "I know."

Tink gave Lily's hand a squeeze.

Lily's heart sank. She knew Tink meant to be comforting. But Lily knew what that little squeeze meant.

The worst was still to come.

8

Rani returned with several other fairies. Some carried blankets and a clay thermos full of hot tea. Others had come along simply to see what the fuss was about. Ree, the fairy queen, was with them.

"What has happened?" Queen Ree asked.

The two harvest-talent fairies repeated their story.

When they were done, Vidia pushed her way to the front of the crowd. "That vile plant has caused nothing but trouble in Pixie Hollow. It should be cut down!" she cried.

Some fairies in the crowd began to murmur, "She's right. The plant is bad. We should get rid of it."

Lily stood with her hand on the plant's stem. Her heart pounded in her chest. Would they try to uproot the plant right then and there?

Suddenly, Tinker Bell moved over to stand beside the plant, too. She folded her arms across her chest and glared at Vidia and the grumbling fairies.

Lily gave her a grateful look. She knew Tink didn't care much for the plant. But Tink was a good friend. And a brave one.

Just then, a familiar face moved through the crowd. It was Iris. She came to stand next to Lily, Tink, and the plant.

"This is Lily's garden. The plant belongs

to her. You can't just chop it down," Iris declared.

"That's right," said another voice. It was Rosetta. She joined Lily, Iris, and Tink. "This plant has my protection," she declared.

"And mine!"

"And mine!"

More garden fairies came out of the crowd. They gathered around Lily and the plant. Now there were two big groups of fairies facing each other. And everyone looked angry.

"That plant is a menace to all fairies!" Vidia shouted. "Pell and Pluck could have been caught by an owl this morning."

More fairies raised their voices in agreement.

"It's not the plant's fault they were flying in the dark without a lamp!" a garden sparrow man argued.

"That plant is ugly!" cried a light-talent

fairy.

"It's a monster!" added a cooking-talent sparrow man.

"*You're* a monster. Plant hater!" a garden-talent fairy snapped back.

"Petalhead!" the sparrow man retorted.

Suddenly, another voice rang out like a bell.

"*Fairies!*"

Everyone turned to look. Queen Ree was standing with her hands on her hips. She glowered at the crowd of fairies before her.

"What a disgrace. This is *not* how we settle a disagreement in Pixie Hollow," said the queen. Her voice sounded cool, but her gaze was stern. Behind her, the queen's four attendants glared at the crowd. "Shouting. Name-calling. I'm disappointed in all of you," the queen declared.

Several fairies in the crowd hung their

heads. Vidia lifted her chin defiantly.

"At noon tomorrow we will have a meeting in the courtyard of the Home Tree," said the queen. "All fairies are to attend – that includes you, Vidia."

She fixed the fast-flying fairy with a steely look. Vidia was known for disobeying the queen's commands. Vidia tossed her hair as if she didn't care. But the look on her face said she understood.

"Everyone will have a chance to speak," the queen continued. "Until then, I want all fairies to return to their fairy domains. Now."

Grumbling, the groups of fairies broke up and left.

Lily flew over to Pell and Pluck. "Let me help you carry some raspberries back to the kitchen," she said.

"I think you've done enough," Pell snapped.

"First the wasps, now this," Pluck added.

"From now on, we'll get our raspberries somewhere else," said Pell.

Lifting their chins, the two fairies turned their backs on Lily and flew away.

Lily's heart sank. No one would enjoy her garden as long as the plant was standing. But after taking care of it so lovingly, how could she bear to cut it down?

For the rest of the day, no one was happy. Despite the queen's commands, the fairies couldn't seem to get along.

When a weaving-talent fairy tried to collect sweetgrass to weave her baskets, the garden fairies snubbed her. The cooking-talent fairies argued with the harvest-talent fairies, and as a result, no one got any lunch. Hungry and cross, a light fairy snapped at a water fairy. The water fairy splashed her, and soon the light fairies and the water fairies weren't speaking to each other. Each talent group was annoyed with the other.

Lily stayed away from the Home Tree. She spent the whole day sitting in the skimpy shade of the mysterious plant. And after a lot of thinking, she came to a decision.

"If the fairies of Pixie Hollow decide that the plant should be cut down, I must not stand in their way," Lily told herself. It pained her to say it. But she knew that the most important thing was keeping the peace in the fairy kingdom.

"I only hope they don't make me do it," she added. Lily had never swung an axe in her life. She didn't think she would be able to.

Just then, Spring, a message-talent fairy, flew quickly into the garden. She landed next to Lily.

Spring seemed to be out of breath. She took a couple of deep gulps of air. "I have a message from the queen," she managed at last.

Lily nodded and waited.

"The meeting has been changed. All fairies are to meet in the courtyard at sundown," Spring explained.

Lily's eyes widened. But it wasn't only because of the message. Something strange was happening behind Spring's head.

A yellow fruit the size of a gooseberry was growing from one of the plant's branches. And it seemed to be getting bigger before Lily's eyes!

"There has been too much fighting," Spring went on. She hadn't noticed Lily's startled expression. "The queen doesn't want to wait until tomorrow to settle this."

But Lily wasn't listening. She gaped at the

fruit. It had already grown to the size of a small grape.

I can't let Spring see this, Lily thought. *She'll tell the queen, and then the plant will be cut down for sure!*

Quickly, Lily jumped up. She whisked her daisy-petal sun hat off her head and hung it over the rapidly growing fruit.

Spring turned to face her.

Lily smiled innocently. "Courtyard at sundown," she repeated. "I'll be there." She was eager to get Spring out of her garden as quickly as possible.

Spring nodded. "Good. Well, I'm off. I've got to get the message to the rest of the fairy kingdom. If you see anyone, you'll be sure to let them know?"

"Yes – oh!" Lily gasped. Out of the corner of her eye, she saw another odd fruit growing from a branch nearby.

"What is it?" Spring started to turn.

Lily sprang into the air, blocking Spring's view. She hovered there, dramatically clutching her foot. *Think fast*, Lily told herself. "I mean – ow! I just stepped on a pine needle!" she exclaimed.

Spring looked at the ground. There was no pine needle in sight. In fact, there wasn't a pine tree anywhere near Lily's garden. She gave Lily a curious look.

"Well, then, see you tonight," Spring said.

Lily nodded. "Fly safely," she sang cheerily.

When Spring was gone, Lily breathed a sigh of relief. Then she stepped back to look at the plant. Yellow fruits with bumpy skin were growing from all its branches. They got bigger and bigger before Lily's eyes. And, Lily noticed with dismay, uglier and uglier.

Lily clutched her head unhappily. If any-one saw the plant now . . . She couldn't finish the thought.

She glanced at the sun. It was low in the sky – almost time for the sunset meeting. *If I can keep anyone from seeing the plant before then*, Lily thought, *there might still be a chance to save it.*

9

THE SUN WAS sinking on the horizon as the fairies made their way to the roots of the Home Tree. Already the courtyard was in shadow. Light fairies posted themselves all around its edges, brightening the space with their glow.

When all the fairies were present, Queen Ree took her place before the crowd.

"Fairies of Never Land," she declared in her clear and noble voice, "there has never been such a disgraceful day in the fairy kingdom."

"It's that plant!" someone called out.

"The plant! The plant is the cause of the trouble!" more fairies chimed in.

The queen held up a hand to quiet them. "Is the plant the trouble?" she asked evenly. "Or is it the fairies? I wonder. Can you blame a single plant for the unkindness fairies have shown each other this afternoon? If you can prove that to me, we will remove the plant."

The fairies began to murmur. Again, the queen silenced them with her hand. "Every fairy will have a chance to speak. Who will go first?"

"The plant belongs to Lily!" Tinker Bell called out.

Other fairies echoed her. "Yes, it's Lily's. Let her speak first!"

Lily found herself being pushed to the front of the crowd. She had never felt so many fairy eyes on her before, and her heart raced.

She took a deep breath.

"Yes, it's true," she said. "I planted the seed in my garden, and I took care of it."

"What kind of plant is it?" Queen Ree asked.

Lily shook her head. "I don't know. I found the seed in the forest. I'd never seen one before. But I think it's a good plant –"

Again, some fairies began to grumble.

"She doesn't even know what it is!"

"Good? It isn't good for anything!"

The queen waited until the crowd quieted down. Then she asked, "Lily, do you think the plant is the cause of all the trouble in Pixie Hollow?"

Before Lily could answer, a voice suddenly shouted, "Wait!"

Everyone turned to look as a breathless Iris flew into the courtyard. She was carrying a yellow object the size and shape of a lemon.

"Wait! Wait!" Iris cried again. She landed on the ground in front of the crowd of fairies. "Everyone, look! The plant grew fruit."

All the other fairies crowded around to see the strange fruit.

Only Lily stayed where she was. She buried her face in her hands. The secret was out. Now there was no chance of saving the plant.

"What is it?" the fairies murmured. Lily sneaked a look at the fruit. The bumpy, ugly skin was gone. Now it had a pearly sheen that almost seemed to glow. Curious, some fairies reached out to touch it.

"Careful!" someone cried. "It might be poisonous!"

At once, the crowd drew back.

"It's not poisonous," Iris said. "And what's more, I know what it is."

Everyone, including Lily, looked at her in surprise.

"Well," said the queen, "what is it?"

Iris smiled mysteriously. "Come with me," she said.

With Iris leading the way, all the fairies of Pixie Hollow set out for Lily's garden. Soon they saw the strange plant.

Several fairies gasped in surprise. The plant's branches were heavy with clusters of round, golden fruit.

Iris turned to one of the light-talent fairies. "Fira," she said, "will you and your fairies give us some light?"

Fira and the other light-talent fairies brightened their glows. They surrounded the plant, covering it with their light.

"Ah!" the crowd of fairies sighed. The golden fruit glowed in the light. The plant looked very beautiful.

"Now watch," said Iris. She flew up and grasped one of the fruits. Using all her might, she gave it a tug. The fruit came away in her arms.

Immediately, another fruit grew in place of the one she had just plucked.

Lily's hand flew to her mouth. The fairies around her gasped. Even the queen looked stunned.

"What is it?" she asked again.

"I'll show you," Iris replied. She set the fruit on the ground and opened her book. She held up a page. On it was a drawing of a tree. Its drooping branches were full of round, glowing fruit. The drawing was labelled "Ever Tree" in Iris's handwriting.

"It flowers only once, then grows fruit forever and ever. That's why it's called an Ever tree," Iris explained.

"Can you eat the fruit?" the queen asked.

Iris asked Tink for her dagger. She split

open the skin of the fruit she'd picked.

Inside were golden pips, not unlike the red ones of a pomegranate. Iris plucked a pip out and popped it in her mouth. "Yes," she said as honey-coloured juice dribbled down her chin. "It's delicious."

Several fairies reached for the pips. Iris handed one to Lily. When she bit into it, it tasted like ice-cold lemonade on a hot day. Satisfying and perfect.

"But how did you know what it was?" Lily asked Iris.

"I heard about the Ever tree a long time ago," Iris explained. "So long ago that I'd almost forgotten about it. Of course, I drew the picture as it was described to me and wrote down everything I heard.

"Many, many years ago, before there were any fairies here, Ever trees grew all over Never Land. Then the volcano on Torth Mountain erupted and all the trees burned. Every last one.

"There was only one Ever seed known to be left," Iris went on. "But the dragon Kyto selfishly hoarded it in his collection of rare treasures."

At the mention of Kyto, several fairies shuddered and looked towards Torth Mountain, home of the dragon's prison lair. Kyto was wicked through and through.

"But how did the seed get here?" Tinker Bell asked.

Iris shrugged. "I guess it blew out of his lair. If Lily hadn't found it and planted it so carefully, Never Land might never have seen another Ever tree. Ever trees are very fragile, you know. They need lots of care."

Everyone turned to look at Lily.

She ducked her head shyly. "Iris helped," she said simply.

Several more fairies had clustered around the fruit and were gobbling its pips.

"I could make a delicious tart out of this juice," said Dulcie.

"This fruit would make excellent jam," said Pell. Pluck nodded.

Even Vidia was eating the Ever fruit, though she quickly hid it behind her back when Lily looked her way. But a moment later, she shrugged and pulled it out again. "It's good," she said grudgingly, and went back to eating.

More fairies began to pull fruit from the plant's branches. Suddenly, Queen Ree cried, "Stop!"

The fairies froze. They looked at the queen, startled.

"This plant belongs to Lily," said the queen. "It's up to her whether she wants to share it."

All the fairies turned to Lily.

Lily looked around at them and grinned. "Of course I want to share," she said. "Everyone is welcome."

The fairies cheered. And they spent the rest of the night eating Ever fruit and dancing beneath the plant's branches.

10

LILY LAY ON a soft patch of moss in the corner of her garden. All day long her garden had bustled with activity as fairies dropped by to pick fruit from the Ever tree. The cooking-talent fairies needed several of the fruits to make a special dessert. The healing-talent fairies wanted to see if the fruit could be used to treat illnesses. And hungry fairies from all the talents came by to get a snack.

Lily loved having all the visitors. But now she was tired. She wanted nothing more than to relax on the moss and watch the grass grow.

She had just spotted a blade of grass that needed her attention when a shrill voice interrupted her thoughts.

"Goodness, what a day!"

Lily closed her eyes and sighed. Then she sat up and said, "Hello, Iris."

Iris plopped down beside Lily on the moss. "What a day I've had!" she declared. "I've been around to five different gardens today. All the garden fairies want me to write about their gardens. I've had to add more pages to my book."

She held up her book, which was fatter than ever.

"And the other fairies! Every little seed they find, they bring to me. They think it's another Ever tree. Of course, they're all just ordinary flower seeds.

"But don't worry, Lily," Iris went on, "I

made sure to save time for you. Now, tell me about your marigolds."

She opened to a blank leaf in her book and set her writing splinter on the page.

Lily frowned, confused. "What about them?" she asked.

"Why, they're so golden! They should be called *more*-igolds, don't you think?"

Iris laughed at her own joke.

And this time, Lily laughed along with her.